THE TRAINING PHASE...

Operation Retribution Part 1

PALADiN SHADOWS SERiES, BOOK 7

A Novel by **Aidan Red**

▲

Edited by Tina Perdue

Published by Red's Ink and Quill, Wichita, KS

For information on other works by Aidan Red, Science Fiction and Fiction, published or forthcoming, visit RedsInkandQuill.com or AidanRedBooks.com

eBook ISBNs:

978-1-946039-18-7

1-946039-18-7

Softcover ISBNs:

978-1-946039-19-4

1-946039-19-5

To my wife for her patience, tolerance and encouragement. Many thanks to my family and friends for their past and continued encouragement and assistance.

The Training Phase...

Greg's new assignment turned into a campaign to take the fight against the slavers to the source, and Shara suddenly found herself a teacher, a co-commander, the leading fighter ace in the newly named Apache Squadron, with responsibilities larger than herself. The slavers continued to step up their attempts to discover the condition of the captured base, Point Obscure, and Shara valiantly shouldered the intensifying, uneasy feelings, the increasing burden of being the only Talent that can sense their coming . Then her cousin's fighter is destroyed pursuing a fleeing intruder and Shara, the only one that could help, launches in desperate flight, an attempt to reach her before it is too late.

Chapters

Seventy-Six   1
Seventy-Seven   19
Seventy-Eight   37
Seventy-Nine   55
Eighty   73
Eighty-One   91
Eighty-Two   111
Eighty-Three   125
Eighty-Four   143
Eighty-Five   163
Eighty-Six   181
Riggin Town Map   198
Riggs Valley Map   199
Glossary   201
Books by Aidan Red   215
More Books by Aidan Red   216
About the Author   217

Seventy-Six
Galactic date: C.3482.361

"Chairman Sorgat," Merchandise Director Korveel said in Galactic Standard as he entered the large, circular office. He walked around the teardrop shaped conference table, and stopped beside the oval desk at the back of the room. Korveel looked at the Traders Union's senior chairman through the haze of the holographic information display screen suspended at one side, above the uncluttered desk. "I was told you wished to see me."

"Yes, Director Korveel," the chairman said as he looked aside from the columns and rows of data slowly scrolling up the screen. The scrolling stopped as the chairman turned his attention to the merchandise director. "I do not seem to have an update from Terran Operations Director Ahaar since his communiqué on 3482.353. That was eight standard turns ago."

"Nor I," Korveel said as he straightened his posture. "I have sent a number of inquiries, but have not received any replies."

"Do you not think that that is odd?" the chairman asked, "especially since he owes us a status on his collection and transfer of the seed families to the new terran launch facility."

"It could be," Korveel continued, "that he is busy executing your commands."

"Humph," the chairman muttered, unconvinced. "Has he resumed any form of shipments?" He raised his eyebrow and stared at Korveel.

"No," Korveel admitted. "He has not shipped anything, perishables or non-perishables, since Point Obscure was presumed attacked on 3482.315." He hesitated and watched the chairman's expression. "Rumor has it, sir, that Warlord Prince

1

Kiese is displeased at the interruption in the shipments of slaves."

"Yes," the chairman admitted and looked back steadily. "But why would there be rumors, Korveel? Why should he not be displeased? Our shipments have been regular and on time for over three thousand turns. He and other customers have built their progress, and in some cases, the expansion of their influence, based on our rigorous and trusted schedules. Why would anyone be displeased when those shipments simply stop? Why should there be..." He stopped and glanced at the screen above his desk, then looked back at the merchandise director and pursed his lips in thought.

"Since Director Ahaar is not returning queries made to his terran command center, and we cannot contact Point Obscure, you must contact someone at the new launch facility's construction site," Director Sorgat said. "There has to be someone that knows what Director Ahaar is doing and what the construction progress is." He waited.

"Sir," Korveel said, lowering his voice slightly. "We have also not heard from the troop ships sent at Director Ahaar's last request to secure the area around Point Obscure. They were due to arrive in terran orbit on 3482.355 with instructions to drop a landing party of over a thousand ground support marines and three hundred fighters for top cover protection."

The chairman's mouth dropped open as he stood up behind the desk. "And no word I presume? No mission status? No—"

"None, sir," Korveel admitted firmly with a slight shake of his head.

"I told him to stop his irrational pursuit of Point Obscure," the chairman said, half to himself, "that it would take care of itself by waiting. But did he wait? No! He brought in an attack fleet complete with an invasion force to investigate Obscure's silence. I told him if he continued, his actions would attract attention and our operations discovered. The attack on Point Obscure was bad enough, but now he has cost us how much more? Two freighters sent to transfer his seed families, a couple dozen agents sent to investigate what has happened there, their drop ships and escort fighters, and now a total of five battlecruisers, over a legion of Marines and hundreds of fighters?" The chairman slowly turned and opened the sashes covering the windows behind his desk. "I presume they are gone," he said as he surveyed the vast expanse of Casha-Six's sand desert beyond the windows.

"It would seem so, sir," Korveel continued with soft resignation, "and it would also seem that Director Ahaar successfully attracted someone's attention."

The chairman's shoulders drooped noticeably. "So it would seem, Korveel. So it would seem."

"I will try to make contact as you suggest," Korveel said in a more upbeat tone.

"Yes," the chairman said in return. "We will need to explore other, less obvious means to gather intelligence on the status of Point Obscure and to restart those shipments. Have the Council prepare their choice for Director Ahaar's replacement."

"I will report as soon as I know something," Korveel said and waited. At the chairman's nod, he retraced his steps across the conference room and closed the door behind him.

Thursday, December 8

Terra

The lead trooper of the two man reconnaissance team, dropped remotely to search and investigate the situation surrounding Point Obscure, reached out in the darkness and stopped when he touched the wide trunk of the huge pine tree. He caught the second trooper's arm and pulled him close to kneel beside him.

"A rest," the leader said in Galactic Standard. "Eat and rest quickly. We are very short on time."

"It has taken us three local turns," the second agreed as he opened a food pouch and pulled out an energy bar. "Two more than expected. Whoever picked this route did not survey it well."

"Yes, noted. Climbing down that eastern escarpment was more difficult," the leader admitted. "Topography mapping was too coarse to identify the three separate, sheer drops. It was not good that we lost a full night and half a turn just getting down to the valley floor."

"Only to spend the next turn and a half crawling through this heavy undergrowth," the second said with displeasure and took a sip from his belt canteen.

"We should be close," the leader said as he shielded the dim light of his notepad and checked their progress. "But, it is the twenty-first par of this turn and if we do not find anything in the next four, we must divert to the large lake. Pick up is in eight pars and we cannot be late."

"Do you have a meteorological forecast?" the second asked as he stowed his rations and canteen. "Ambient temperature is falling and the humidity indications are rising."

"There was no forecast available," the leader said with a sigh that barely covered the disgust in his voice. "And the weather is very changeable in this place. We cannot break our silence to ask for an update." He growled, almost under his breath. "Nothing about this mission was planned properly."

"I only have enough pack power for another par of cloaking," the second said as he stood up beside the leader and noted his indicators.

"Myself also," the leader admitted and switched his cloaking transmitter off. "Save power until we see something."

"See something?" the second laughed. "It is so dark my dark vision equipment cannot see. Are we still progressing in the correct direction? My global positioning power failed last nightfall."

Without responding, the leader moved forward and groped his way farther into the omnipresent murk. He continued without conversation, intentionally not mentioning the foreboding he was feeling as he monitored the nearly depleted power indication along the left edge of his night vision goggle's view.

About a par later, his notepad flashed in its pouch, its soft beeping catching his attention.

"Veils up!" he said sharply. "I have sixteen targets in a wide half circle ahead of us."

"Sixteen?" the second questioned as he activated his cloaking transmitter.

"Move to our left," the leader said and pushed his second in that direction. "Find suitable cover at a distance from this spot."

Quickly, they moved and, nearly to the advancing indications, they found a large, fallen tree trunk. Crouched behind the trunk, the leader consulted his notepad again.

"This arm is nearly upon us, still moving toward us slowly," he said and tapped the screen. "The half circle seems to be closing on our previous position."

The second rose up and tried to see over the log, but the darkness prevailed; nothing was revealed in his goggle's view. Then suddenly he slapped the transmitter on his utility belt.

"My veil has failed," he said, louder than he had intended. He slapped the transmitter activation pad again, but nothing changed.

The leader cursed and then his veil also failed.

"Ungood! They can sense us now," the leader said with resignation. "Use the pad display and try to make a hole in their line. Go for the lake!"

The leader jumped up, turned in the direction of the southern blips on his pad and began spraying the darkness with hand laser fire. The second followed suit. Someone yelled in the darkness; a hit. Encouraged, the leader pressed forward. He barely recognized the streak that shot back and burst in a brilliant flash beside him. He did not see his second fall into the underbrush. He continued, firing blindly into the darkness. The second streak was the last thing he saw.

▲

"Seventeen," the Peace Force surveillance technician said softly when he tapped his ear and heard the gentle static. "The two targets to our east just uncloaked. They are six miles out."

"Path?" Galactic Peace Force marine Seventeen asked in response.

"Their present track will take them about a mile and a half south of Obscure," the technician said.

"Keep watch. I'll alert USL15," Seventeen said and terminated the connection. He recomposed his thoughts and then tapped his ear again.

"USL15. Update from Surveillance," Seventeen said.

"Kiile here. What do they have?"

Seventeen relayed the information.

"Okay, they're about one and a half to two hours out," Kiile said as he planned his next moves in his mind. "Contact Twenty. Have half his squad meet me on the east side of the launch portal in fifteen minutes. We'll go out and meet them. Shut down all exterior lights and have Launch Bay Control close the launch portal. Squad Leader Kiile out."

He turned his attention to the Q-Ships parked outside and tapped his ear again. "Major Mooren, Squad Leader Kiile here. The two interlopers are less than six miles east and heading slightly south of us," Kiile said giving him a status. "I will accompany a squad of fifteen and we will arrange a pincer to surround them. I would like one ship for air cover."

"MKCC5 is available for close support air cover and we will take TTYF8 up to keep the drop ship from engaging," the major replied. "I will advise Major Kooich."

⟁

Galactic Peace Force Major Crem Mooren and Lieutenant Franni Kaal were already on board their recondite class corvette, heavy fighter Q-TTYF8, a Q-Ship in the familiar jargon of the Force, when the lights around the launch bay portal and all internal launch bay lights went dark. They could feel the soft rumble of the portal panels closing as the ground vibration came up through the landing struts of the Q-Ship. From his place in the pilot's cushioned chair, he glanced over his shoulder to his nav-com lieutenant seated in the navigation-communications compartment just aft of the cockpit and the central compartment.

"Okay, Franni," Major Mooren said. "Give MKCC5 the details and let KKLC14 know we're going up for the drop ship. Cloaking on."

"Ignition ready, Major," she remarked casually as the check list scrolled before her on one of the many display screens in the nav-com compartment. "Cloaking on, sensor blocking on, shields are active."

"Thanks Franni," the major said as he began to lift TTYF8 through Obscure's shield barrier.

"Looks like the weather is going to get nasty," Franni said absently as she swept her attention across the display screens and felt the first of the weather's turbulent bumps.

"Can you broadcast the maintenance diagnostic codes STSX gave us?"

"Yes," she answered as TTYF8 displayed the sequences, beginning with the codes for the Mark Twenty-Five mass cloaking transmitters. When nothing showed up on the scanner display, she repeated the next one down the list in her mind, then the next. "Got it," she said proudly as the blip appeared on the scanner with the Mark Twenty-One codes.

Way to go, girl, the major said to himself as he pulled TTYF8 into a near vertical ascent. "TTYF, give me a heads up display of the target and display the range and closure velocity on the pilot's screen."

Franni turned and looked at the back of Major Mooren's cushion chair, wondering if she actually heard him praise her. She had heard his thoughts only a few times before and wasn't certain she had this time. And even though he was trying to live up to his word and be a better team player, paying more attention to their mutual needs as a flight crew, an actual complement would also be a first, even if he just thought it.

He swung TTYF8 south of the drop ship, circled around in the climb and slowly leveled at the same orbital altitude before he glanced back. "Franni set your consoles to voice commands and come forward please."

"Major?"

"Yes, please," he confirmed as he reached out and unlatched the jump seat on the right hand cockpit wall. "I think TTYF will follow your voice commands if you're up here as well as he will if you're back there."

She drifted up beside him and twisted around to strap herself into the seat.

"I asked Major Kooich," Crem said, "how Casi learned so much so fast and he said he thought it was a combination of her being an extremely talented student and that the colonel always shared what he was doing with her."

He smiled at her as he eased TTYF's nose to the left to center the blip within the heads up display's reticule.

She saw he was smiling from ear to ear as she took in the view from the cockpit for the first time; she was not just looking at a bank of consoles and displays. She was pleased at the change in his manner after their conversation last week in Obscure's Mess, after his stated commitment to making them a team and not just a crew.

"See if you can drop their cloaking with that diagnostic command trick that Major Kooich and Leeana told us about," Crem asked without looking away from his targeting display.

Franni had TTYF display the sequence they had received from STSX1 on the cockpit monitor and when she read it in her mind, she suddenly felt a surge of sincere pleasure. She quickly looked at the major's profile and saw he was still smiling. Then she looked through the canopy and saw the small glint in the distance.

You've got the knack, girl. You certainly do, she heard him say to himself, then he turned and smiled at her. "Niccly done, Lieutenant. Very nicely done."

She smiled back at him, realizing that she did actually *hear* his thoughts. She was glad she was finally able to *hear* someone again, but it was also troubling; she knew it was the first step toward an intimacy that she wasn't sure she was ready for. Her thoughts warred with themselves, knowing that to be truly in sync and the best they could be required they be *linked* to each other, but she was afraid. *Linking had not been enough when LLGC15 was destroyed... It had not been enough to keep my major alive...* She shook her head sharply. *Stop it! That was nearly two years ago, and you've got to move on! You have new responsibilities! Stay focused!*

"TTYF, Shields Full, forward and left side," Major Mooren said, his voice bringing her back to the moment. "I'm bringing us around so they'll be on our left," he said for her to hear.

She watched the glint take form and remembered the ship's shape from the profile files TTYF had in archives.

"TTYF, set up a broadside volley from all three turrets," he continued, glancing at her to be sure she was all right with what she was seeing. "At one mile I'm going to drop our visual cloaking and give them a moment to consider surrender. But they won't and our shields should protect us."

She stared at him, his last two comments hung ominously in the space between them.

"Okay, TTYF," he said, focusing his gaze on the ship off their left beam. "Drop visual only. Left shields full, sensor blocking on. Give them a hail."

Suddenly the space between the two ships filled with faintly visible cannon tracks and the drop ship vanished in a brilliant flash and a boiling cloud of smoke and debris. In a heartbeat, the ship was gone.

"Are you okay?" Crem asked as he swung TTYF around and started their descent. *'I must admit you did good... You did really good. You didn't even flinch.'*

"Yes. Yes, I think I am," she said and looked away as a smile slowly spread across her face.

▲

9

TTYF8 was on approach to Obscure from the south when they heard Squad Leader Kiile's call to MKCC5.

"They've cloaked," Kiile said. "Can you light them up?"

A moment passed without a response.

"MKCC5? We're going to lose them." Kiile's voice in their headphones sounded stressed.

"We aren't getting any response," Lieutenant Donnr's voice said.

"Lieutenant Donnr, this is Lieutenant Kaal," Franni said, quickly interrupting the communications. "What codes have you tried?"

Lieutenant Donnr responded with the list of GPF codes.

"Try the Corsecain code," Franni suggested.

"I'm... I'm not finding that one," Lieutenant Donnr's frustrated voice answered.

"It's your mission, but do you mind if I try?" Franni pressed.

"No ma'am. Please."

When Franni turned to the display beside the major, she was surprised that TTYF8 had already placed the code phrase on the screen between her and the forward cockpit bulkhead. She broadcast her thoughts and quickly read the phrase to herself. She smiled when the two blips popped onto the scanner display.

'Stellar, girl. Absolutely stellar.'

She looked down at the cockpit floor and smiled at the major's comment.

"We've got them. Thanks," Kiile's voice said and switched off.

Saturday, December 10

"STSX," Lieutenant Casi Geaardt said as their home world,

10

earth, cloud dappled and mostly blue, steadily grew ahead of them. She quickly scanned the navigational displays. "We're about a hundred thousand miles out. What are the local weather conditions at the ranch?"

"STRONG NORTHWESTERLY WINDS AND HEAVY SNOW," the Q-Ship's central computer answered, "SLOWLY ABATING AS THE MORNING PROGRESSES. AMBIENT TEMPERATURE IS FOURTEEN DEGREES FAHRENHEIT, MINUS TEN CELSIUS. CURRENTLY FOURTEEN INCHES OF NEW SNOW ACCUMULATED, AN ADDITIONAL SIX INCHES ARE FORECAST."

She turned her head and looked over her shoulder at her husband quietly watching from the new, more comfortable right hand side jump seat.

"I think I'll land at the ranch," she continued. "I'd rather not open STSX's lair with all of the blowing snow."

Colonel Stran Geaardt smiled at her, proud of how she handled STSX and the situations that arose on their missions. He was profoundly proud of his five foot tall, raven haired tomboy mate in every way, completely captivated by her beautiful face, her figure, her husky voice and especially her passion and eager, confident spirit. He was also extremely pleased with the Peace Force director's acceptance of her rapid training and capabilities, awarding her with her Pilot's ribbon and a grade promotion to upper-lieutenant, along with numerous Meritorious Conduct ribbons and Distinguished Service Stars. Casi was the fastest rising star in the Galactic Peace Force's history, the very first ever accepted into the Peace Force as an officer, an under-lieutenant, which was an unheard of before accomplishment, as well as achieving full Pilot status and Q-Ship qualification in a matter of weeks. To say the least, the director was 'very' taken by his newest Shadow.

"I think that's very prudent," he remarked, then turned to the ship. "STSX, send a message to Major Kooich."

The message display illuminated, suspended in the space before him to the right of the pilot's cushioned chair and the message heading coalesced on it.

"SCRAMBLE"

"C.DATE 3482.363 LOCAL DAY 344, 0835 HRS
TO: Q-KKLC14; MAJOR HENCH KOOICH; RWKR17-SC
FROM: Q-STSX1; COLONEL STRAN GEAARDT,
HQZL09-ES."

Stran pulled his thoughts together and composed his message, happy knowing that Casi was listening.

'PRESENTLY INSIDE LUNAR ORBIT. ARRIVING AT HEADQUARTERS WITHIN THE HOUR. PLEASE ADVISE MATTI AND HANK, AND PLAN TO MEET US IF YOUR SCHEDULE ALLOWS. CASI WILL ALERT KKLC14 WHEN WE ARE ON APPROACH. EOM.'

"You said you wanted to meet with Kiile and Jim when we got back," Casi reminded him without turning.

"Yes, I did," Stran agreed, "but let's see where everyone is and what's been going on before we call a meeting and get everyone together."

"INCOMING MESSAGE."

"Read it, STSX," Stran said in response.

"C.DATE 3482.363 LOCAL DAY 344, 0840 HRS," STSX's masculine voice said out loud as it repeated the contents of the message.

"TO: Q-STSX1; COLONEL STRAN GEAARDT, HQZL09-ES
FROM: Q-KKLC14; MAJOR HENCH KOOICH;

RWKR17-SC

GOOD TO HAVE YOU BACK HOME. WE WILL GREET YOU WHEN YOU ARRIVE. STSX WILL NEED TO TRANSMIT THE ATTACHED ADMITTANCE CODES ON APPROACH. KIILE HAS INSTALLED SHIELD GENERATORS TO PROTECT THE RANCH STRUCTURES AND LANDING AREAS AND A SHIELD GENERATOR AND A CLOAKING TRANSMITTER TO PROTECT THE LAIR. EOM."

"Thanks, STSX. It sounds like they've been busy while we were away," Casi said as she adjusted the navigational display.

"Certainly does," Stran agreed.

⁂

With carrysacks in hand, happy to be back on the ground, Casi led Stran out through STSX's aft portal and down the ramp. At the bottom, she stopped, smiled and looked at the familiar ranch, their refuge, now gaily decorated with Christmas lights stretched along the back eaves. She wondered if the grey morning light was playing tricks on her eyes, the gentle wind and lightly falling snow was contrary to STSX's report. She turned to Stran and looked up at him in question.

"It's the shields, love," he said, almost causally. "The shields are keeping most of the wind and the heavier snow out."

"Well, I'll be," she said softly as he nudged her toward the back porch and the heavy door into the coat room.

Major Kooich and Leeana got up from the dining room table when Casi pushed the heavy wooden door open and surprised them both. Leeana hurried around the table and caught Casi in a tight hug.

"It's good to see you back, Shara," Leeana said, smiling at Greg.

Shara smiled, caught slightly off guard; it was the first time anyone had called her by her actual, terran name in over a week. She grew up as Shara Smallwood and now Shara Malone for just under two months, married to Greg Malone on Sunday, the 13th of November.

Major Kooich extended his arm and Greg grabbed his forearm in greeting. "Safe trip, Colonel?" he asked as Greg dropped his carrysack beside Shara's in the archway between the coat room and dining room.

"Very good trip, Major," he admitted with a wink. "I have some things from the director to pass along, but I think I'll wait to explain the details when we can get the group together. By the looks of the weather, that might not happen until tomorrow or Monday."

Shara smiled at his wink and felt her face warm with the memories of their incredible trip to the director's meeting and the Commendation Ceremony in the Rings, dining and dancing in the Royal Mess and the equivalent of nearly six days with just the two of them on board STSX enroute; an indescribable belated honeymoon. Then she turned to the kitchen and pushed the door open and called, "Matti, Cara, Annie?"

When two women came out of their quarters and into the kitchen, Shara greeted them with a hug, and then looked around, "Where's Annie?"

"Pantry," Matti, her head house girl said and pointed to the door across the room.

Shara hurried to the door and slowly pushed it open. When she saw Annie rearranging can goods with her back to the door, she said, "Caught ya!" and when Annie spun in surprise, Shara hurried forward and hugged her.

When they stepped back into the kitchen, she smiled at each of them. "Thanks for taking care of the place for us, and for putting up all of the decorations. What a nice surprise." Then her expression took on a conspiratorial air. "You know I've mentioned that Greg and I fly places and have a ship?"

They nodded slowly.

"Well ladies," she said with a wide smile, "you haven't had the opportunity before, but if you'll look out back," she gestured to the mud room door, "you'll get to see what Greg and I fly. Go take a look, so you'll know I've not been kidding you."

Shara pushed them through the doorway and watched and listened as they stared at STSX setting quietly in the pasture, only a few yards beyond the house.

"I know I don't need to remind you," she said softly, "how necessary our secrecy is, but our ship and Major Kooich's ship will be coming and going quite often from here, and I want you to be comfortable with seeing them. Just like you've become comfortable seeing our remotes coming and going."

"You really fly that, Mrs. Shara?" Matti asked, surprise still coloring her expression.

"Yes Matti," Shara said and touched the Pilot's ribbon just below her left shoulder on her form fitting blue-black body suit. "Now, both Greg and I are his pilots."

▲

Back inside the kitchen, Shara turned to Annie. "Now that we've upset your morning routine, would it be possible for you to throw something together for a hot breakfast?"

"Certainly Mrs. Shara," Annie replied. "It'll only take a few minutes."

"Thanks Annie," she said and smiled at each of them as she returned to the dining room.

Major Kooich and Leeana had sat back down on one side of the table and Greg had settled in one of the chairs he and Shara normally used nearer to the kitchen.

"Where're Nick and Jill?" Shara asked as she sat down and poured herself a cup of coffee from the carafe on the table. Then she turned to Greg, "Annie's fixing us something."

"Jill followed Nick out to his apartment—" Leeana was saying when the back door swung open and Jill burst into the room, Nick a close step behind her.

"Shar! You're back!" Jill squealed, her long red hair bouncing as she hurried around the table to catch Shara half up out of her chair. "Leeana said you were nearly here, but we didn't hear

STSX land. We figured you'd be going to the lair first." After a long hug, Jill caught Shara's shoulders and pushed her back to look at her. "Let's see what's different," she said, looking down at Shara, her eyes scanning the ribbons and lapel insignias. "A different ribbon here," she pointed, "and a different one on your lapel."

"Pilot's ribbon and another promotion," Shara said softly.

"Full black bars," Leeana said in surprise. "You were upped to an upper-lieutenant? And a Space Pilot?"

"Sorry, Leeana," Shara said, looking around Jill. "I know you've worked longer and harder than I have, but—"

"No, Shara. Don't be sorry," Leeana said as she came around to join them. "I think it's wonderful. You've accomplished so much and I'm glad the director has rewarded you for it."

"Can I say hello as well?" Nick asked as he stepped up beside Shara and Jill, interrupting the serious tones that were beginning to surface. "I haven't seen my future sister-in-law in over a week either."

Shara turned and gave Nick a hug as Jill turned to Greg.

"Good to have you back, brother," Jill said and hugged Greg. "I've missed you."

"What? With Nick here to keep you in line?" he said with a smile. "I've missed you too, sis. How're your folks?"

"Like always," Jill explained. "Mother's having a hard time keeping the secret that we're alive and our father's keeping busy with his financial duties at the mill and helping Kiile at Obscure."

"Helping Kiile?" Greg looked at her and then at Major Kooich.

"Kiile's inventory specialist," Major Kooich said softly, "was killed when they intercepted two drops two days ago. TTYF8 got the drop ship. Jack decided to fill in until Kiile gets a replacement."

Greg sobered his expression and nodded 'thanks.' "So stopping Ahaar didn't stop the interlopers."

"Obviously not," Major Kooich said.

"But," Leeana added, "we haven't seen any more fighters in orbit."

"Thanks for small favors," Shara said and turned as the kitchen door opened.

"Mrs. Shara?" Matti called softly. "Your breakfasts are ready."

"Thanks Matti," Shara answered and then to the group. "I presume you have all eaten already, so we're going to eat in front of you while you bring us up to speed on what's been happening here."

Paladin Shadows: The Training Phase...

Seventy-Seven

Special State Deputy Wally Lima, assigned to Riggin when the long time sheriff and his six deputies disappeared in late October, left the Riggin Police Office on his way to make his before-lunch rounds north of the Deerskin River. He had managed the day's heavy snow, the low visibility and the strong winds with enough success to get Carole Davis, to work at Hap's Place by eleven and to get himself back to the office to check on Kenny, the jailer, before starting his rounds.

None of the jail cells were occupied and with no need to have the dispatcher's console manned, Wally let Kenny take an early lunch while he checked the mill and the few businesses north of the river. He felt things had quieted down a little since the confrontation at the bank on Thanksgiving evening and his ill-timed search for the source of the 'bright light' seen by a few on thirty September. That search had confirmed, in more ways than one, that the missing people were indeed being stolen, kidnapped and pressed into servitude by an organization simply known as the Family and controlled by what was left of the Reeds family's Council of Elders. That search had also reintroduced him to his connections with the Galactic Peace Force and the fact that their agents were present here in the valley, a heavily guarded secret about which he and Carole now shared knowledge.

Wally was headed back east on Mill Road, the Rusty Saw Bar and Grill just faintly visible ahead of him on the left through the dense, blowing snow, when his jeep began to pull toward the plowed snow bank along the road, unresponsive to his steering input. He stopped and opened the driver's side door. The howl of the wind overwhelmed all other sounds and the horizontal snow cut his useful vision to mere feet. He checked the driver's side tires and then worked his way around the front of the jeep to the passenger's side. There he found the flat front tire.

Wondering how it had gone flat since the tires were only a few weeks old, he stood up and slowly started to the back to get the tool kit and spare tire mounted there.

Something suddenly hit him in the back, hard! It slammed him against the side of the jeep; his head bounced as a second something crashed into his skull and his knees folded. He fell back, unconscious into the snow bank.

⋏

Greg and Shara had settled in their customary manner in the overstuffed chair in the living room by the fireplace with Shara sitting crosswise on Greg's lap. Major Kooich and his mate Leeana had taken the longer couch to the side away from the fireplace and Nick and Jill the love seat facing them.

"So you're saying," Shara continued, "that Franni is showing a talent for lighting up cloaking transmitters?"

"That's what I hear," Major Kooich said, "from Major Romaan and confirmed by Major Mooren. She helped Lieutenant Donnr when MKCC5 couldn't find the Corsecain codes to support Kiile."

Greg held his conflicted thoughts to himself. "How is Major Mooren doing?"

"Very well," Major Kooich said, noticing Greg's controlled expression. "You knew I left him and TTYF8 in charge when we went after Ahaar."

"Yes, and I'll admit I was concerned by your choice," Greg said, "but the choice was yours and now it seems that it was the right one."

"Thank you," Major Kooich said with a smile.

"I was concerned his original arrogance might become a liability," Greg admitted.

"I think your talk with him," Leeana said, "and Shara's talk with them after they wandered away from their duty station and left the space station unguarded helped a lot. Kiile said

Seventeen also had a talk with both of them one day in the Mess about your and Shara's roles in getting us where we are."

"About us?" Shara questioned, surprised.

"Certainly," Leeana said as if it should be obvious. "Kiile says Seventeen is one of your most loyal fans, along with most of his marines. He apparently felt Major Mooren needed to show more of the respect you two deserve. Obviously the major had said something that Seventeen felt could be misinterpreted."

Shara looked at Greg, still puzzled.

"Since you have been gone," Major Kooich continued. "Major Mooren and Lieutenant Kaal have made noticeable improvements. I wouldn't have known anything about Franni's assistance if Major Romaan and Kiile had not informed me. Major Mooren only confirmed it when I specifically asked."

"Then they are learning some self-control," Greg said.

Shara suddenly twitched at the image that flashed through her mind, the barest of an instant before Greg saw it.

"Five says Wally's been shot!" Shara shouted as she stood up.

Greg rose with her and looked at Major Kooich while his mind queried STSX for a status of Kiile's men.

Shara turned to Jill, "Both of you get your Blues and meet us in STSX. You can change there."

"Major?" Greg asked quickly. "Is KKLC in the lair?"

"Yes," he answered. "We have one of our remotes here."

Shara turned to Greg. "Let's take STSX. We can drop down from hover and with the four of us we can get Wally into Medical."

"Major?" Greg asked again. "You're welcome to join us in STSX. Kiile and his men can't get there as quickly as we can."

Major Kooich looked at Leeana and saw her nod.

"We'll get our Blues and meet you Colonel," Leeana said as they followed Nick to the back door.

Shara looked at Greg as they followed the others out. "He's ignition ready and powered up."

▲

Greg swung a cloaked STSX around to place the extended ramp as close to Wally as he could. Shara stood in the open aft portal and helped guide him.

'That's close, love,' she said in her mind. *'Down about another six feet.'* Then she changed her focus, *'Jill, you and Nick take Four and Six and get Carole. I'll let you know if we're done before you start back.'*

'Got it!' Jill replied silently, then slipped her jeans and jacket over her Blues.

Nick followed her out of the aft portal, fully accepting that Shara and Jill had silently discussed the details without him hearing what had been said.

'Stay cloaked,' Shara reminded Jill as they mounted the two remotes and disappeared into the snowy haze.

Greg and Major Kooich were already lifting Wally by his arms when Shara and Leeana joined them and each took a leg.

"He's alive," Major Kooich said as they lifted him.

"Medical is up and waiting," Shara said as they carried Wally through the aft portal and up the aisle.

Greg and Major Kooich worked Wally's jacket off as Shara checked his bloody head.

"Looks like something sliced his scalp," she said and daubed the gash with a cloth. "No bone penetration. Leeana, get me that clotting salve from the bin," she continued, absently gesturing to the cabinet at the foot of Medical.

"Five said he was hit in the back," Greg added as he tossed Wally's jacket onto the opposite couch.

"No blood, Colonel," Major Kooich said as he looked at Greg. "What's the jacket show?"

Greg stopped mid-turn at the major's comment and retrieved the jacket.

"There's definitely an impact tear in the leather outer," Greg noted as he studied the back of the jacket, "but no penetration."

He felt the bulk of the jacket and glanced at Major Kooich. "Looks like some form of ballistic lining. He may have broken or cracked ribs."

Major Kooich felt Wally's back and finding nothing specific, he laid Wally down on Medical's couch and secured Medical's arm band. His familiarity born of years in service, he quickly keyed the console above Wally's head then stepped back and watched the clear cover rotate closed over the couch.

Suddenly he looked at Greg. "Sorry, Colonel," he said with a sheepish smile. "I didn't mean to over-step—"

"You're fine," Greg said and held up his hand. "No need to apologize."

"STSX?" Shara said out loud. "Close the aft portal and take us to hover over Hap's."

▲

Carole Davis had just finished serving a table near the front of Hap's dining area and was heading back to the kitchen serving window at the end of the long, wooden bar when she saw Jill and her bright red head of hair peek through the back door. Jill quickly slipped inside and stopped at the opposite end of the bar, motioning with quick gestures for Carole to come.

Surprised to see Jill out in public, especially alone, Carole set her tray on the ledge and went to her.

"Get your coat," Jill whispered firmly and tugged at her own coat to be sure Carole understood.

"What? I can't leave, Jill," Carole said, confused.

"Carole," Jill said firmly as she caught Carole's arm and pulled her close. "We think Wally's been shot! Now get your coat!"

Carole's face went pale. Quickly, she collected her coat and told the other waitress that she had an emergency, but when she turned to the door, Jill had already stepped out and no one else seemed to have noticed she had been there.

▲ ▲ ▲ ▲ ▲

The snow covered figure, wrapped in a heavy, thigh length coat, insulated pants, boots and a wool head mask, stomped up onto the front porch of the house on the northwest corner of Birch and Mann. With the barest of knocks, he pushed the door open, slipped in quickly and closed the door as he jerked his knitted head mask off.

The two men at the dining room table turned in casual greeting.

"Where have you been, Pat?" the unshaven man asked and took another sip of his beer. "Weather is not fit for man n'r beasts."

"Just took care of some overdue business, Ben," Pat said as he shed his coat and hung it on a peg beside the front door. "Payback for my brother, Pete."

The two men stopped talking and watched Pat for a long moment.

"What do you mean 'payback?'" the second man asked, holding Pat with a curious stare.

"What d'ya mean, Abe?" Pat asked in answer. "You know my brother was with the guys on Thanksgiving when that deputy stopped them down by the bank. There were six of them and no one's seen any of 'em since."

"Yeah," the unshaven Ben said. "I heard they were going to try and jump that deputy just for spite. Something about him being too inquisitive."

"You say the deputy got them instead?" Abe chuckled. "Serves 'em right."

"Well he may have got my brother and the other five," Pat said with a smirk, "but I just put two thirty-eight slugs in him, Ben. He will not be asking any more nosy questions."

"You did what?" Ben jumped to his feet.

"I stopped his nosing around," Pat said and stood straight with his shoulders back.

"Shit!" Abe said and slowly uncoiled from his chair. "You shot a state deputy! Now we'll have another deputy, or maybe a couple of new deputies sent up here to see what's going on! The state will over run this place. Don't you ever use your head?"

Pat's smile slowly faded. "But my brother—"

"To hell with your brother!" Ben shouted. "Your brother and the others got what they went looking for. Trouble! And if the deputy took them in, they will have to deal with it!"

"But Pat," Abe said smoothly, trying to hold his temper, "Elder Dave Barns and Don Nikle were working the issues to convince the deputy there isn't a problem, and possibly get him to see the council's side of things. Maybe even get him to help, either knowingly or unknowingly."

Pat's face went pale.

"And now, Pat," Abe added, "your stupid revenge has just dumped the apple cart again! Shit! I don't know what they'll do when I explain what you've done to Elder Dave. I guess I should ask you if he's dead and if anyone saw you."

"Should be and no," Pat said firmly. "I was hidden just above the river, west of Main and the snow was blowing too hard for anyone to see. The wind even covered the sounds. But I didn't stay around to check his pulse."

Abe turned and tapped the Mountain Phone Company terminal when the front and the back doors suddenly burst open.

⚔ ⚔ ⚔ ⚔ ⚔

Wally was sitting up on Medical's couch between Shara and Leeana, Major Kooich and Greg on the opposite couch talking with him in low voices when the aft, inner portal opened and Jill led Nick and a pale and wide eyed Carole into STSX's sleeping area. Carole focused on Wally and quickly hurried past

Jill and knelt in front of him.

"Are you okay?" she asked, grabbing his free hand, startled to see him sitting up. Her expression showing it.

He smiled, holding a cloth on the side of his head. "Yeah, I'm okay, thanks to our very good friends that kept me from freezing to death."

She looked up at Shara and then to Leeana, remembering her from their forced stay at the secret facility in the woods and then again at Shara's ranch. "Thanks. How'd it happen?"

"He was ambushed," Leeana explained as Shara got up and slipped past her to talk to Jill. "Up by that bar north of the river. Looked like someone shot a tire and forced him to get out so they could get a shot at him. Didn't penetrate his jacket, though one of the shots grazed his head."

Carole smiled, "His jacket. He gave me one when that guy shot at us out by that place... I think you called it Obscure." Leeana nodded and she continued. "He said they were the latest in bullet-proof fashions. Thank goodness they work."

Carole looked around, smiled at Greg, Major Kooich and Nick, but stopped when she saw Shara don her wool head mask.

"Major, could I suggest you get Carole a container of ration tea?" Greg said as he got up, turned to the central compartment and disappeared up the rungs attached to the wall.

The aft portal's inner panel opened and Shara and Jill stepped into the airlock.

"Where are they going?" Carole asked, turning back to Leeana.

"Remote Five followed the man that shot Wally," she explained. "Shara and Jill are going after him and the colonel is going to follow them from here, giving them top cover if they need assistance."

Carole's head seemed to spin. "Where is here? When Jill brought me on that, that... remote she called it, we rose up above Hap's and were suddenly face to face with a doorway that appeared out of thin air."

"It's a little unnerving the first time," Leeana admitted as the aft portal slid closed. "We're in their ship and the colonel is going to fly above them. The ship is cloaked so you can't see it until you're very close."

⋏

"Do you have your headband?" Shara asked Jill as she slipped her head mask on, referring to the vibrant red cloth headbands that she, Jill and Rose had worn when they attacked Ahaar's data collection facility.

"Yes. I keep mine in my pouch so I'll always remember those killed or stolen and why we're doing this."

"When we get down and in position, masks off and headbands on," Shara said with a devious smile. "There are three of them and I want them to remember what we look like." Then she turned her thoughts to Greg. *Five says they're in a house on the northwest corner of Birch and Mann. Far east end of Birch above the college. I'll take the front and Jill will take the back. Four and Five will provide cover for the back and Six will cover me in front.*

'We'll be close, just above you, Bren,' Greg said.

She smiled as they mounted the remotes, very pleased whenever Greg called her by the nickname he gave her just after they met and before they were married; Bren, short for BrenCara, his 'special raven haired friend.'

'Okay, Jill. Let's show them what we think of people that try to hurt one of ours,' Shara said in her mind as they stepped onto their remote's stirrups and started their descent.

⋏

Shara had directed Five to stay with Four and to not let anyone out of the backdoor as she stepped off Six's stirrup onto the front porch. She knew when Jill stepped off Four onto the back stoop then turned her attention to the three inside and listened to their heated conversation.

'Headbands on,' Shara said to Jill as she tied hers in place.

'Remotes are On Station and Greg is above us.'

'I'm ready,' Jill answered.

'Kaasprs ready. On my count, kick the doors open. One. Two. Mark!'

Shara kicked the door latch and dove in as the door banged open. The three men started to turn at the noise, but stopped suddenly when the backdoor also burst open. Shara yelled for them to get on the floor and grabbed the one that had admitted to doing the shooting. The heavier, unshaven man spun at Jill and tried to grab her, but Jill sidestepped and slammed her fist across the back of his neck. He collapsed head first in a dazed pile as Jill held the second man at bay with her outstretched hand and the Kaaspr aimed squarely at his head.

Shara caught her man by the throat and swept his feet out from under him, smashing him face down onto the floor. "I SAID to get down on the floor!" she shouted and shoved the Kaaspr against the back of his head. "Hands behind your back!"

She quickly snapped a wrist cuff on him and turned to help Jill with her two, but stopped when she realized Jill had them both face down on the floor and had the first cuffed.

Shara smiled at Jill, pleased at how well she had implemented Kiile's teachings. Then she got up and knelt down beside the man in the middle of the group.

"Jill, watch the other two," she said as she pulled him up, shoved him back against the wall and covered his face with the palm of her free hand. She tightened her grip, closed her eyes and linked with STSX.

'STSX, I want them to remember we were here and the red headbands, not who we are, and I want them to tell the Elders we came because one of them tried to kill Wally Lima and that we will instantly deal with anyone that harasses or attacks Wally Lima in the future, his friends or any of the deputies that are assigned to him.'

When STSX had finished and the man slumped forward, Shara got up and turned to the unshaven man, rolled him over and covered his terror filled eyes with the palm of her hand.

'Same message, STSX.'

When she had finished with the unshaven man, Shara asked, *'STSX, can Jill hear you?'*

A long moment passed and STSX replied, *'ONLY IF SHE MUST HEAR.'*

Shara chuckled, realizing Jill wasn't STSX's choice. *'Okay, I'll remember that, but you will have to speak to her in the future. I may have to have her try the scans. Do a mind scan.'* she said with a sigh as she lifted the last man toward her and clasped her hand over his terrified face, her thumb and second finger squeezed his temples firmly.

Shara settled into a rigid position and let STSX pull the man's memories through her until the man quivered and slumped in exhausted silence. Her body also sagged and she slowly forced herself to ignore the images that tried to cling to her when the information flowed to STSX.

Jill was quickly beside Shara, softly talking to her to bring her back to their 'now.' She had witnessed Shara do the mind scan twice before and shuddered at how draining it was for her.

"Remove the cuffs on those two," Shara said weakly, "and let them wake up on their own. They have a story to pass along to the Elders. We'll take this one to Kiile."

C.3482.364

"Chairman Sorgat," the aide's voice said through the interoffice communications link.

"Yes," the chairman answered when he glanced down from the data screen floating at the side of his desk.

"I have a message from Intelligence Services for you," the aide explained. "Playback is available through Link Four."

"Thank you," he said absently and selected the link. "Play," he said when the link beeped 'ready.'

"Chairman Sorgat," the recorded voice started. "I am

Director Libtn of Intelligence and we have gathered some information through our informant network. I have received a coded message from one of our agents that we placed within the Galactic Peace Force. The agent obtained a verbal tip that the Peace Force recently held a ceremony honoring six fighter crews on 3482.358 and during that ceremony at an undisclosed location, one of those crews was honored for the capture of a Traders Union's data collection facility, the removal of a Traders Union director and the destruction of two battlecruisers and numerous fighters. The incident date was the same as the loss of your two cruisers, 3482.353.

"At this time we do not have any information on the particular crew or where they are based, but it seems evident, or at least highly probable, that the Peace Force was responsible for the loss of the cruisers and fighters you mentioned. I will alert you if we get any further information concerning the crew responsible."

The message ended and the chairman stared at the communications console, his mind full of new questions. If Director Libtn was right in his suspicions, then Director Ahaar was the director removed and his terran data center was the captured facility. That would certainly explain why Director Ahaar had not replied to the communiqués sent. And if his data center was the captured facility, then it stood to reason that the Peace Force had also captured his collected data.

The chairman cursed loudly, stood up abruptly and began pacing back and forth behind his large desk. He knew that if the Peace Force was in control of the terran facilities, they were also likely in control of Point Obscure. He continued pacing, realizing it would be nearly impossible to continue shipments from the humans' home planet.

Nearly, but not completely, he told himself, trying to force something positive out of the gloomy prospects. Something had to be done to collect as many of the perishables they could before...

Before when? he asked himself and keyed the communications console for Director Korveel. As the merchandise director, he should have some ideas on how they could still collect and ship their needed humanoids. Then he wondered if they could try just one more time to sneak a reconnaissance scout in and see anything usable.

Sunday, December 11

Greg slowly nodded to each member of the 'Team,' as Shara called them, as he looked at them seated around the informal living room. He thought the Christmas tree by the dining room and the colorful decorations added an odd counter point to the business at hand. Lieutenant Jim Woods, his father Bill Woods and his grandfather Gary Woods, now CEO of the Woods Mill and Lumber Company, had arrived together, risking the perils of the blowing and drifting snow to get here. Upper Squad Leader Kiile had arrived by remote from Obscure with Greg and Jill's Dad, Jack Thomas, minutes behind Jim and the others. Paul Hawkins, Shara's grandfather's brother and owner of the Rockin' H ranch to their north had come early and joined him, Shara, Major Kooich, Leeana, Jill and Nick for lunch. Only Rose Mitchell and Doug McIntire were absent.

"I guess I should get started," Greg said as he stood beside Shara sitting in their favorite over-stuffed chair, his back to the fire in the fireplace. "Thank you for coming, especially in this weather."

"At least the snow stopped last night," Jim said, smiling as he looked at Greg.

"Certainly helped a lot," Greg agreed. "A few things came out of our trip that I need to pass along. The first two things I will mention are that Shara, or Casi to be more specific, was promoted to upper-lieutenant and she now has the distinction of being a full-fledged Space Pilot and she is a fully qualified Q-Ship pilot."

Shara forced herself to keep her composure and not shy away from the complement in Greg's explanation and the congratulations of those in the room.

Kiile smiled and clapped at the news. "Knew you could do it. Quicker than anyone."

"Thanks, Kiile," Shara said.

"And that brings me to the first item on my list of changes that I want to implement in this campaign." Greg stopped a moment, smiled and looked at Major Kooich. "Major, I want each and every nav-com trained as a Cadet Pilot, and as quickly as they can complete the syllabus provided by the director, he will evaluate them. If we are successful, they will be awarded Pilot's ribbons."

Leeana stared at Greg, her mouth slightly agape, completely and happily surprised by Greg's words.

"I thought, Major," Greg continued, "when you and Leeana were attacked, that you could have been injured instead of Leeana, or the pilot of any Q-Ship injured instead of the nav-com. I want both crewmen to be able to fly and fight so if either of them is injured or otherwise incapacitated, the other can continue or execute a retreat."

Major Kooich nodded with a knowing smile. "Is the syllabus available?"

"Yes. STSX can distribute it as soon as you want it," Greg said. "As you know, I have specific ideas on how to implement the syllabus' knowledge, so we'll discuss that in a separate meeting.

"My second item also concerns you Major. You may have noticed, STSX now sports a new Squadron identification. He wears Shara's red headband in the form of a double, diagonal red stripe around his forward, central body. I want all of our transports and Q-Ships, those we now have and those we will get, banded in the same manner with a single stripe. We are the first Peace Force Squadron to take the fight directly to the Traders Union and I want them to know who they're fighting. I will discuss tactics before our missions. We will be getting more fighters and we will be taking the fight off planet. The director has agreed that when other Q-Ships support us in a fight, they will also be banded with our squadron identification."

"Do we have the paint?" Major Kooich asked pointedly.

"In two days, a supply transport will arrive and park in a high orbit," Greg said and looked at Kiile, "and I would like for our Marines to assist us in bringing the supplies and spare parts down. I am told we will have a Class XI transport arriving and Obscure will not be able to handle its length or height. It will have paint among many other things we and Obscure need. And by the way, all female crewmen will have a headband. Shara, or Casi, will have them for distribution." Greg remembered Kiile's remark about a 'Ladies' Brigade.'

"Colonel," Kiile said. "The transport could come down cloaked and hover inside our veil, to minimize the effort involved. It would be a lot easier to unload here without the complications of working in space."

"STSX will give you the communications clearance codes and you may coordinate with the transport's crew and loadmasters to work out the details. Thanks Kiile."

"Thank you, Colonel," Kiile said.

"Major," Greg continued as he looked back at Major Kooich, "along with the supplies, the transport will be bringing four patrol fighters, two Instructor Pilots, three cadet pilots and two mechanics. One mechanic is also Q-Ship qualified."

"Patrol fighters?" Leeana asked.

"Yes, Leeana," Greg said with a wrinkled expression. "It seems the director is testing me. He wants to accelerate the teaching of a group of cadets, specifically pointing to my teaching Shara. So I will have to pull a star out of the helmet and teach the cadets the fine art of combat flying in weeks rather than years. We can discuss my thoughts on training and assignments later, but Paul, I would like your assistance in the classroom."

Paul nodded and smiled, "I'd like that very much."

"I see," Major Kooich said with a chuckle. "Sometimes it isn't good to show off."

"Oh, and the patrol fighters will also get the red band," Greg said, smiling with a nod, but continued without commenting on Major Kooich's lightly veiled jibe. "Now, for those of you not involved directly in managing our fights, I will need your help concerning Wally Lima. I would like the four of you, Jim, Bill, Gary and Paul, to keep watch. Wally is a Peace Force POI, and the director is arranging for a change in his assignment status and additional deputies. Wally is strung out to the point he has little or no time to even sleep."

"What do you need us to do?" Bill asked, glancing at the other three.

"Talk to people," Greg began to explain. "Get a feel for who likes him and who doesn't. He wants to do his job and do it well. Help people understand he is not like Sheriff Black was. He's not here to spy on folks or to tell them what to do. He's here to help keep them safe. He's learning about the Family and knows they are behind the missing people."

"You might not know," Shara picked up the discussion, "but Carole, your sister-in-law Jim, was attacked for being with him. Wally was able to intervene before she was seriously hurt, but then Thanksgiving night, six men attacked him behind the bank at Main and Fir. The group of Kiile's men that were keeping watch over us that night gave him support and aid. The following Tuesday, he and Carole went searching for the source of the 'bright light' and they were attacked just northwest of Obscure by Seth Clotter. Wally killed him in the exchange.

"Seventeen had them escorted to Obscure and held until we finished with Ahaar, so he knows about this group, Greg, Jill, Nick, myself, Kiile, Major Kooich and Leeana. He knows there are others, but we haven't identified any of the rest of you. Then yesterday, Pat McClure shot Wally twice with a thirty-eight caliber pistol, but Wally was wearing his proper protective gear and is doing fine. We were able to collect Pat and we've tried to send a message to the Elders through two of his acquaintances."

"We have to get the town behind him," Greg said when Shara paused, "And you're the best ones to start changing public opinion."

"We'll do what we can," Gary said. "I like Wally, but I wasn't aware of the problems he's been facing. Talking is one thing I can do."

"Thanks, Gary," Greg said and then turned to Kiile again. "I need to hold an assembly at Obscure to pass out a few commendations the director has awarded. How soon can that be arranged?"

"Tomorrow?" Kiile asked, thinking sooner would be better than later. "0900?"

"Very good," Greg agreed and looked at Major Kooich. "I want your assignees to attend also, Major. Jill, you and Nick in clean Blues. And would you see that Rose and Doug are there? Also in their Blues."

Seventy-Eight

"Come in," Wally said loudly when he heard the knock on his front door.

Stretched out in the recliner in his sparsely furnished living room, he snapped to full alert when the knock interrupted the quiet of the late afternoon. His hand dropped to the holster and pistol hanging beside the chair, his fingers curled around the grip.

"Hey," Carole said as she slipped in and quickly closed the door behind her, hoping she did not let in too much of the winter cold. She shed her coat, folded it and laid it on the floor beside the front door, then crossed the room and stopped beside the recliner as he set the back upright. She noticed him pull is hand up from beside the chair before he reach up to her.

"Come here, you," he said with a wide smile.

"How're you doing?" she asked and caught his hand. She looked around and tried to decide if she wanted to sit on the floor beside him or get a folding chair from his dining room. "You have to get more furniture."

Before she could decide, he turned her and pulled her onto his lap. "I was hoping I would get to see you today."

"Wally! I shouldn't be on your lap," she insisted and tried to get up.

"Stay where you are," he insisted. "I'm fine supported by the chair. You heard Shar. I only have a couple of cracked ribs and whatever they wrapped me with is doing a great job of keeping things in place."

"But I don't want to—"

"Stop," he said gently and pulled her to him. He kissed her

softly and took his time releasing her. "This is much better medicine than sitting in this chair by myself. How was your work today?"

She let herself relax against him and laid her head on his shoulder. "The work was okay, but I was worried about you."

"Why? I'm okay."

"Wally," she said softly, "you are, again. This time." She tilted her head, still on his shoulder, to look at him. "I'm scared that the next time you won't be."

Wally thought in silence for a long moment. "I know it's hard to think things will get better, but I do think they will. And I know this is hard on you and I'm sorry for causing you so much worry. I was so pleased that Jill and Nick went and got you. Talk about being surprised."

"I'm scared, Wally," she admitted, her voice just above a whisper. "The last weeks have gotten worse."

"I know," he said, trying to decide if what he had been thinking about was the right thing to say. "Carole, I'm really caught in the middle here, but I only know of one way to keep you from being so concerned or scared that something will happen."

She lifted her head and looked at him. "What?"

He looked at her and took a deep breath. "The only thing I can think of is for you to stay away from me. Maybe the Family will leave you alone and you can stop worrying about me."

"You don't want me to be here?"

Wally sighed and looked into the concern he saw in her eyes. "That isn't it, and you know it," he said, unsure of how to proceed and squeezed her shoulders. He could not lie to her. "I've rehearsed what I should say to you, but it always gets tangled up when I try to put it into words. It's not about what I want, Carole, but yet, it is. I want you to be safe and to not worry, and you're not safe when you're around me."

She laid her head back down on his shoulder and thought to herself for a very long moment before she spoke again.

"We're both being silly. I'm safest when I'm with you. I know you want me to be safe, but you forget that you are why I'm safe. My problem, my worry, is that I can't help keep you safe. I don't know how. I don't know what I can do. I'll worry if I'm here with you and I'll worry more if you send me away."

"Carole," he admitted, "I can't do my job and always be safe. I can only hope my job will change for the better."

"I know," she said softly and buried her face against his neck. "And I will still worry because I care about you."

He turned her head and kissed her again. "I really don't want you to be anywhere else."

"Me either," she said, then pushed herself up and looked at him. "So, Wally, I think we should dwell on happier things. I talked to Hap today."

"And what was the topic of his historic event?" he teased.

"He hired two new girls to wait tables so I negotiated Sunday and one other day in the week off, but I still have to do eleven to midnight the rest of the week. You have to help me pick my second day off."

"That's great, but that's also a big hit financially for you," he said, torn between the idea of the better schedule and the lesser hours.

"Oh," she smiled at his concern, "He's agreed to a fifteen percent raise and no tip sharing."

Wally smiled at her. "Wow. Maybe not such a big hit after all."

"I wanted the time off more than the money," she said brightly. "And you, Mr. Lima, when you get some additional help, are going to take planned days off too." Then she slipped off his lap and stood up. "Do you have anything around here that I can fix for dinner?"

"Sure," he said to both proposals. "I have steaks, chicken, some left over pulled and sliced pork, a little venison, potatoes, peas, corn, French cut green beans, some frozen asparagus, breads, rolls, various pastas, ingredients for sauces and a number of things I can make for deserts. I'm sure we can figure out something. What are you in the mood for?"

Monday, December 12

Stran was pleased with how the commendation ceremonies had gone. They had landed and parked STSX1 at the west edge of the clearing south of Obscure's launch portal and entered through the portal hatchway and down the curved corridor of steps into the Launch Bay; the route brought back vivid memories. As the campaign commanders, in their dress Blues with all of their assorted ribbons, braids and stars, his and Casi's entrance had affected the proper respectful response from the Q-Ship crews and even Kiile's marines.

He began the ceremony by awarding Major Kooich and Leeana each a Campaign Lieutenant Commander ribbon, a Campaign medal and Meritorious Conduct ribbons. Then he awarded each of them a Wing Leader ribbon with a Braid of Distinction. Then with Major Kooich's assistance, he had addressed the four Q-Ship crews and in turn had awarded them each with Campaign medals and ribbons for Meritorious Conduct in the Face of the Enemy. When Stran had finished with his and the major's direct reports, he turned the ceremony over to Upper Squad Leader Kiile to distribute the package of medals and ribbons Stran had brought from the director. Each of his marines received a Campaign medal, but Kiile was selective in how he awarded the Meritorious Conduct ribbons, Braids and Distinguished Service Stars.

When the ceremony concluded, Stran and Kiile jointly dismissed the assembly and Stran led Casi, Major Kooich and Leeana down to the Mess where Kiile had arranged for coffee, tea and an assortment of pastries, which Kiile mentioned were not as good as Annie's sweet breads. Stran took the opportunity for him and Casi to greet each of the crews and then each of Kiile's Marines personally, engaging in congratulations, small talk and listening when they had an idea or a comment they wished to mention to their commander. He was pleased to see Jill, Nick, Rose and Doug engage in casual conversations with the crews and Marines as well.

Stran and Casi had just finished a short conversation with a young marine when Stran noticed Major Mooren talking with Major Kooich near the Mess entrance. Major Kooich was nodding and seemed pleased when Major Mooren turned, followed by Lieutenant Kaal, and approached him and Casi.

"Colonel, if we may," Major Mooren said as he stopped. "We would like to thank you and the lieutenant," he nodded respectfully to Casi, "for your guidance and tolerance. Franni and I and Major Miiles and Lieutenant Meecia have to get back upstairs. It is our turn, but again, we wanted to take a moment to say thank you."

"You are very welcome, Major, Lieutenant," he said and extended his forearm to each of them in turn.

Casi grasped their forearms as well before they saluted, turned and left the Mess.

"Well, Colonel?" Major Kooich asked when he stopped beside him and Casi.

"I think, Major," Stran replied, "that your choice in a wing second was a good one. They both seem to take the responsibility very seriously."

"Yes, they do," the major agreed, "thanks to the two of you." Then he smiled at Stran. "Of course, serving under the most highly decorated and well thought of Shadows and campaign commanders, does help instill a bit of awe and pride in the members of the squadron."

Leeana chuckled at Casi's abashed smile.

"With that, Major," Stran said and smiled at Casi, "I will leave the festivities with you and Leeana. We'll see you back at the ranch for a late lunch. I have something to discuss with our four non-combatants and I would like you and Leeana to be there when I do."

⚔ ⚔ ⚔ ⚔ ⚔

Deputy Wally Lima bent over his desk, searching another set of links concerning the missing people, hunting for their family members, any that might still be living in the valley or still in the state. He was certain there was some way to tie them to his attackers on Thanksgiving and yesterday to families that had missing members. Somehow, he wanted to see if he could see a pattern and predict who might be a potential problem, a potential risk, or a potential threat.

He had just sent a new list of possibilities to the printer when the sound of three car doors closing reached him from the parking lot behind the office. He got up and went to the printer and stopped, turned so his right hip and free hand were hidden from anyone entering the back door. He wanted to be ready if it was another surprise.

The door swung in and a man wearing tan slacks and a state deputy's jacket stepped in. Two others, similarly dressed, followed him in and closed the door.

"Wally Lima?" the first deputy asked. When Wally nodded, the deputy continued, extending his hand to greet him. "I'm Deputy Thomas Baine, friends call me Thom, and these two are Deputies Dan Lupis and Ted Marks. We've been assigned to you here in Riggin. I understand you've been having a little trouble."

Wally shook each of their hands, not certain he was hearing them correctly. "You've been assigned here?"

"Yes," Thom said as he pulled an envelope from his inside jacket pocket. "I have a letter for you from the Department of State Law Enforcement in the Capital. It should explain everything."

Wally took the envelope, tore it open and removed the letter. A smile slowly crossed his face and he glanced up at the three of them.

"I can certainly use the help," Wally said and gestured to chairs at the other six desks. "Before I start explaining what has been going on, have you made any arrangement for places to stay?"

"Not yet," Dan said as he pulled a chair from the nearest desk and sat down. "We were given the names of yourself, a Jack Thomas, Bill Woods or a George Hattle to contact."

"Very good," Wally said. "Those are the names I would have given you. Do you prefer separate accommodations?" When they nodded, he turned to the phone console, selected the speaker on and keyed Bill's code. When the connection completed and the voice on the other end said "hello," Wally continued. "Bill, this is Wally Lima. How quickly can you find separate houses or apartments for three new deputies?"

"How quickly do you need them?" Bill asked.

"They have arrived and need places, temporary at least until you or George can find something permanent. Jack is tied up and can't help right now, so I'm asking you to see what you can find."

"Give me a little bit and I'll get back with you," he said. "Oh, are you in the office? Or are you going to be out?"

"I'll be here until lunch, then I'm meeting Carole at Hap's," he said. "After that we'll be making the early afternoon rounds. I'll take the deputies with me. Kenny's planning on an early lunch so he'll be here while I'm gone."

"Okay," Bill said and the connection terminated.

Wally grinned and leaned back in his chair. "Gentlemen, we have a very interesting and precarious situation here in Riggin. Here's what I know, what I've learned since I got here and what I think we are faced with."

Wally spent the next three hours explaining what he knew, learned and thought. He discussed how he came to be assigned in Riggin, how a group of southern valley people were responsible for manipulating and coercing people, the suspicion around the numerous missing persons, how the town came to be divided, scared and afraid of his presence. He discussed the ranching interests and how the ranchers tried to keep to themselves and handle their own problems, the tact they would need when they offered assistance and the hesitancy of the ranchers to accept it. Though he carefully explained the northern valley's nature, he was careful to not mention or allude to the parallel existence of the Peace Force and the numerous abettors.

▲

When Wally led the three Deputies through Hap's front door and crossed the dining area, every conversation stopped and the patrons watched them as they made their way to the bar. The people knew Wally, but suddenly saw four deputies. Carole greeted them when they paused at the bar and he gestured for her to join them.

He quickly introduced Thom, Dan and Ted to her and her to them and asked if they could get a table. Carole seated them near the kitchen side of the bar and gave them menus to review. When she came back, she set Wally's mug and a carafe of coffee on the table and took the drink orders from each of the three.

"Guess she knows what you like," Thom said with a grin, and turned Wally's mug to look at the deputy's star.

"Yes, she does," he said without rising to the questioning tone. "We are together. There are a few places to eat in town. Jerry's, two blocks down, has breakfast, lunch and dinner. The Rusty Saw up north of the river, is pub-grub, lunch and dinner and is more to the liking of the mill workers. Hap's Place, here, is pub-grub and a few specialties for lunch and dinner and is the local college hangout. Since Carole and I have gotten together, I try to take lunch here. Connie's Deli up on Main, next door to Sally's Casuals and across the street from our office, is a breakfast and lunch place and the Stone Fence Steakhouse, up on Lynx Creek, is true to its name, lunch and dinner. Otherwise, it's home cooking or ninety or so miles down to Clay. As I was explaining before we came in, most of the folks here are good folks, but there is an underlying tension, a fear and a threat that will seem to jump out when you least expect it."

"Like yesterday?" Ted asked, "When someone, out of the blue, tried to kill you?"

"Yeah," Wally sighed. "Those are the ones I'm trying to figure out. There has to be a way to figure out and understand the emotions, the reasons behind why some people are willing or driven to act that way."

"What will you have?" Carole asked, interrupting Wally's explanation as she set the two coffee mugs and a water glass on the table.

When she had taken their orders, Wally stopped her a second. "Carole, whoever did this great mug for me should be asked if they could make one for each of our new residents. They may drop in occasionally and I wouldn't want them to feel slighted."

She smiled. "I'll see what Mel can do."

When she had gone, Ted asked, "We were told this is timber and horse country. Are there any extracurricular activities that you can tell us about?"

"Here in the north valley, it's basically horses, cattle and a little timber," he began to explain then realized what Ted was actually asking. Glancing at the others, he said, "Well, it's a fairly normal college town, Ted, with one cinema house, two bars, each catering to a different crowd. We have a weekly paper of sorts that has a listing of community events, and gatherings, including a few minor columns concerning items of public interest. We keep a copy in the office.

"After you've been here a little while, you'll discover that the women outnumber the men, significantly. Those of suitable age mostly want honest men and honest relationships, whether they are casual or long term. The boys and men around here, both high school and college, seem to think they have the upper hand and they have an attitude. Get to know the people, young and old, and don't let yourselves get into a situation that compromises your integrity. By nightfall, they'll all know you're here. The town is small and everyone talks. Try to only give them good things to say."

45

▲ ▲ ▲ ▲ ▲

When they had finished lunch, Greg and Shara settled in the casual living room beside the fireplace. Shara moved the footstool to the side of Greg's chair and sat down. Nick and Jill joined them and took the loveseat, and Doug and Rose took the overstuffed chairs near the foyer when Major Kooich and Leeana took places on the longer couch.

"You said you had something you wanted to talk to us about," Jill said, when they were seated.

"Yes, I do, Jill," Greg said and looked at Shara before he continued. "You and Nick told us that you wanted to learn to do what Shara and I do. And Rose, you and Doug implied as much when you came forward to help with the attack on Ahaar's complex. I must admit, as I've said before, that you four are an asset to the team. Jill, Rose, you were both an invaluable help to Shara when we captured Ahaar's complex." Then he turned to Nick and Doug, "You two, though a little rough around the edges, were a big help in both the capture of Obscure and Ahaar's complex. I should have insisted on giving all four of you some training first, but there really wasn't time."

"Thanks," Jill said with a smile and glanced at the others as they nodded.

"When we attacked Point Obscure," Nick said before Greg could continue, "I had no idea what we were getting into. All I could think of was that Jill was being held captive in there somewhere. I wasn't thinking properly about the broader scope of the mission. I think I even argued with you about that."

"Thankfully, for us and for Jill, you survived to learn what we are getting into and what it means. You were much better in the attack on Ahaar's complex, more focused and a real help." Greg smiled at Nick's sheepish grin.

"Thanks."

"In our second meeting with the director," Greg continued,

"we discussed where I intend to lead this campaign and what I think we can accomplish. And part of that discussion included the topic of my current staff and changes that we want to make."

Jill held her questions, knowing Greg would just tell her to be patient and listen first.

"I need a small team that is close to me and Shara, and Hench and Leeana, to help with our personal protection. One's that I can count on when everything seems to be falling apart. I gave the director my list and he reviewed STSX's logs of my critiques and comments that I keep on each individual," Greg said. "He also reviewed Shara's logs and from reading both, the director made some specific suggestions and offered to help."

"What kind of help?" Jill could not resist asking.

"The director agreed that you four are assets and with the proper training, he further agreed with my intention to include you in my small team. The director has offered to provide you with the training materials the Peace Force Academy uses," Greg said, with a slowly growing grin as he saw their mouths slowly open in surprise.

"So you can study here," Shara added, "and not have to go to the Academy for the basics. Some of the material is much like our college courses were and some cover the more physical aspects for being a Shadow."

"The point is," Greg said, his tone more direct. "The director is offering each of you the individual opportunity to become cadets. To actually join the Peace Force and learn what the other cadets learn as well as what I feel you need."

Mouths still agape, they just stared at him and Shara.

Jill finally found her voice and weakly asked, "We'd continue the training we're doing with Kiile's Marines, and learn what they teach at the Academy? We'd be training here, and not away like Meg is?"

"Yes," Greg admitted. "But there will be differences. Like I explained yesterday, the director expects me to teach everything in less time than the academy takes."

"Father was just asking me when I was going to get back to my college classes," Jill said with a sigh. "I'll bet he won't think this is the same thing."

"Greg warned your dad that he was going to have this conversation with you," Shara said. "But you will need to sit down and talk about it with him."

"Yeah, he'll only go to a six on the Richter scale," Jill said and looked at Greg, "but Mother will go to eleven!"

"I don't know what to say about your mother, Jill," Shara said shaking her head slowly, "but your father knows you're not excited by your college major choice."

"Yeah," Jill said, "but to stop and go to work for a policing organization that no one knows exists? I don't see how it'll work."

"Well, Jill," Nick said softly, "Shar did."

Jill looked at Shara. "I don't want this to sound wrong, but you virtually changed everything from your previous life. Don't you feel like you were forced to change?"

"Not really Jill. My life fell apart when my grandparents were killed. 'That' was a forced change. It took me years to get my feet back under me, only to find out my mother was behind it and to see what she thought of me, what she wanted to have happen to me. 'That' was another forced change. It took fighting for my independence and relying on my friends, even one that vehemently disagreed with me and thought I was nuts, to realize I had a say in what was going to happen. We still don't know what will happen when you and I show up in public again," Shara said, "but neither of us are the same girls, Jill. I didn't realize it at first, but I had already met my greatest champion," Shara glanced at Greg and then at Major Kooich and Leeana with a smile. "After Greg saved me from the Trader's poison and I realized how much we meant to each other, I made a choice and Greg and the Peace Force trained me in a new chapter of my life. But Greg and I will maintain the appearances of the other, my previous life of ranching and teaching, and a presence here in Riggin." She inhaled deeply, and looked at Greg. When he nodded, she continued.

"Now you have a choice, Jill," Shara continued. "All four of you do. You have your previous lives to go back to, but those lives have already changed. You've already said you want more, to do what we do, to learn a new aspect of your lives, to learn how to protect our homes. To keep the appearance of your previous life, Jill, you will probably need to finish college and train with the Force at the same time. You'll need to decide if you can live the dual life and you need to discuss what you want with your father."

"Yeah, I know. I really want to do the training," she said and caught Shara's firm expression. "Okay, okay, Shar, I'll talk with father."

"Good," Greg said and then turned to the others. "Nick, Rose, Doug, what're your questions? Objections? Or desires?"

Tuesday, December 13

When Carole and the girls locked up, she was pleased to find Wally waiting behind Hap's. With a quick wave, she got into her jeep and he followed her down the alley and up Baxter to her place and asked if he could come in for a little bit.

Once inside, Carole flipped her shoes off and hung her coat behind the door like she always did, then went down the hall to her bedroom to get comfortable. When she came back to the living room, she found Wally patiently sitting on the couch with an envelope in his hand.

He smiled when he looked up and remembered the night he first saw her wearing the same low cut sweatpants and matching high-waisted sweatshirt top that bared her slender midriff. "You know what that outfit does to me, don't you?"

"Why Wally, what do you mean?" she teased and quickly curled up on his lap.

He pulled her tight and kissed her, letting time slide by without counting. Then slowly, he relaxed and changed the subject. "What do you think? Three new deputies assigned to hopefully make our lives easier."

"I think it's great that you're getting some help," she said, but her tone was not as bright as he expected.

"What is it?" he asked. "What's bothering you?"

"I don't know, Wally," she said softly. "One of the new Deputies seemed odd to me. I don't want to put a damper on how great it is for you to have help, but I guess I feel something isn't quite right."

He thought about her comment for a moment and then he remembered the envelope.

"I'll do a standard background check on them in the morning, but I want to show you something," he said and handed her the envelope.

He held her as she slowly opened the flap, unfolded the letter and read it.

"Marshal!" she almost shouted. "Permanently assigned to Riggin!" She stared at the letter and then looked up at Wally. "Is this real?"

"I'll check it out too, but I think it is," he said and squeezed her.

"It sounds impressive," Carole said, "but how's a marshal different from a sheriff?"

"Sheriffs have a local authority, usually a single city or county," he said with a smile, "but in this state, different than many, a state marshal is the highest rank for a law enforcement officer in the field, and it comes with authority and jurisdiction anywhere in the entire state, in all of the cities and all of the counties."

"But you're going to be assigned here?" she asked, still sounding confused.

"Yes. If I'm reading this right, I'm assuming this is my home base and I'm here for good. As a State Marshal, I'm assigned and won't need to be elected. Maybe the good citizens will accept me and this will really be the assignment I've been looking for."

"God, I hope so," she said and buried her face against his neck, fully surrendering to his embrace.

▲ ▲ ▲ ▲ ▲

Abe and the unshaven Ben fidgeted as they waited in Don Nikle's front room. The drive from Riggin to Clay on the mostly single lane, snow packed highway had been slow, long and silent except for the sounds of the four-wheel drive truck they drove. Don's maid had shown them in respectfully, but said that Don would be a few minutes, that he had expected them earlier and other business had come up. They would have to wait for him. That had been an hour ago.

They jumped in start when the door to the large room suddenly slid open and the older man entered and closed the door loudly behind him.

"You said you had something important to tell me," Don Nikle said as he took a chair and faced the two, his manner irritated by something.

"Yes, sir," Abe said quickly. "It's about Pat."

When Don nodded, Abe continued to explain what Pat had told them about shooting Deputy Lima in revenge for him taking his brother.

"So," Don asked, "he was upset when his brother and his friends decided to confront the deputy for spite, and was further upset when the deputy did his job and took them in?"

"Yeah. We told him his brother was asking for it," Ben said.

Don scowled and thought a minute. "So where is Pat?"

"We do not know," Ben said quickly.

"Strangest thing I've ever seen," Abe began softly. "After Pat told us what he had done and we explained how that'd make you angry, I turned around to call you."

"But you did not call," Don said, adding fact to the

comment.

"No. I didn't get that far," Abe said and looked at the floor. "Two women burst in, kicked the doors open, the front and back at the same time. In a second, the one at the front door had Pat on the floor and cuffed. Ben here, swung at the second, but she took him down with one swing and then turned on me."

"Let me understand this," Don said in disbelief. "Two women took three of you down in seconds? Two men used to brawling and sports with quick reflexes?"

"Yeah," Abe said abashed. "It was over before we knew what'd happened. Pat was out cold and we were staring at the ceiling."

"What else?" Don asked, his tone dry as a desert.

"One of them put her hand over Abe's face," Ben said, "and he went limp. Then she did the same to me and everything went black. I guess I went out too."

Don just stared at them.

"When I woke up," Abe continued, "Pat was gone and Ben was still out beside me. My cuffs were gone and a message was running around in my head."

"A message?" Don asked quietly.

"Yes," Abe said, nodding absently as he spoke. "That we're supposed to tell you that Pat was punished for attacking Wally Lima and that we or anyone that goes against him will be dealt with the same way. The message also said that if the Family persists in trying to control and collect people, or help those that are, they will disappear like the sheriff, his deputies, Judge Bernice, Harry Woods, and Harold Danley, to name a few."

"I had the same message in my head when I woke up," Ben said as he rubbed his forehead and stared at the floor.

"And just who were these women?" Don asked frankly. "What do they look like? Did you recognize them?" Don got up and started pacing.

"No," Ben said. "Not Really."

Don stopped and stared at him. "Not Really?"

"They wore tight fitting dark blue, almost black body suits and a red headband," Abe said, trying to remember details. "But I can't remember their faces."

"Me either," the unshaven Ben said.

"So, Wally has brought in undercover agents to help him," Don finally said. "Well, two can play at this game."

"I'm not sure," Abe said and looked at Don. "Three state deputies showed up today and are being introduced around town as Lima's permanent deputies."

"Who is introducing them?" Don snapped.

"Wally was introducing them," Ben said.

"I thought you said Pat shot him. 'Twice,' I believe you said." Don wrinkled his brow in confusion.

"He didn't look like a man that'd been shot twice," Abe admitted.

"Well," Don finally said and turned to the door. "Anything else this message said to tell me?"

"No," Abe admitted. "But I think they're serious."

"So am I," Don said. "I will discuss this with Elder Dave and see what we can find out about these mysterious women with red headbands."

Seventy-Nine

"Captain," the Peace Force transport nav-com officer said in galactic standard as he turned in his console chair. "I have received a change in arrival instructions from someone identifying himself as a Peace Force Marine, a USL15-EFM."

"A change?" the captain asked as he lowered his chair from his observation dome. "Is it on a legitimate channel?"

"Yes sir," the nav-com officer said. "USL15 says he is the leader of a Peace Force Marine installation on the planet below. He says he is tasked with managing the unloading of our cargos."

"What is the change?" The captain asked as his chair reached the lowest position and he swiveled to face the officer.

"He says Colonel Geaardt," the nav-com replied, "the campaign commander, wants us to descend to their facility, Obscure, and unload inside their veil rather than from here in orbit. We seem to be too large to be enclosed in their launch bay so he asks that we unload from a low hover."

"Is the message properly coded?" the captain asked, concerned by a change in plans that occurred just as they reached the planet.

"Yes," the nav-com said. "The message and codes were authorized and passed by a Q-Ship, Q-STSX1, to USL15."

"An ST Series?" the captain questioned as he rubbed his chin. "Do I remember correctly, that one of the cadets that we have on board was previously assigned as a nav-com on a Q-Ship?"

"I will find out sir," the nav-com said, turned and quickly left the Bridge."

⚔

Captain Cheral Haak followed the nav-com officer after he questioned her and the two other cadets about previous Q-Ship assignments. He was not surprised that she had, since she seriously outranked the other cadets, but nodded respectfully when she answered that she had been assigned as nav-com on a Q-Ship and as an undercover agent on the planet below for three years. She stopped beside the nav-com officer when they entered the Bridge. He stepped aside and gestured for her to proceed.

"Captain, Captain Haak is here," he announced as Cheral stopped behind the dais and faced the back of the captain's chair.

The captain turned and saw she waited comfortably at 'Parade Rest.' "You were assigned here?"

"Yes," she said, at ease speaking with a fellow officer, even if he was the commanding officer of the transport. She proudly repeated her assignment.

"Can you confirm a communiqué that we have received?" the captain asked as the nav com handed her the printout.

"I can try," she said as she read the sheet, smiled at Kiile's identification and then touched her right temple, *'STSX, can you hear me?'*

The response was almost immediate. *'YES CAPTAIN. STSX HEARS YOU CLEARLY.'*

'STSX. I am on the transport bringing supplies and personnel to Obscure. Did you provide Kiile with the authorization and communications information to contact this transport?'

'YES.'

Cheral looked at the captain. "Yes, STSX1 provided the authorizations and codes to USL15 at the colonel's request to make unloading easier than in space."

'STSX, is there space to land the transport?'

'NO. TRANSPORT MUST REMAIN IN HOVER AND FULLY CLOAKED AND SENSOR BLOCKED UNTIL INSIDE

OBSCURE'S VEIL. Q-TTYF8 AND Q-MKCC5 ARE YOUR ESCORTS. THE COLONEL AND LIEUTENANT HAVE SHOWN THE Q-SHIPS WHERE YOU ARE SO YOU WILL NOT NEED TO DROP SENSOR BLOCKING. THEY WILL FOLLOW YOU DOWN TO HOVER. FINAL POSITION DATA WAS UPLOADED WITH THE MESSAGE AND DESCENT AUTHORIZATION IS AWAITING THE TRANSPORT CAPTAIN'S ACCEPTANCE.

Cheral passed STSX's information to the transport's captain.

"We have escorts?" the captain asked, looking at his nav-com.

"Sir, we do not show any ships—"

"They are veiled, sir. And sensor blocked," Cheral interrupted. "And you are fully cloaked and sensor blocked. As STSX said, the commander and his lieutenant are tracking us and directing his Q-Ships. They will stay with us during the descent."

The captain's eyes widened slightly as he looked at Cheral. "So you really are a Shadow."

"Certainly," Cheral said with a slight smile.

"Why are you with the cadets?" he persisted, more curious that he ought to be.

Cheral considered his question and sensed a simple, genuine curiosity. "To gain additional capabilities. Colonel Geaardt has need for pilots, new and old."

The captain blinked and remembered himself. "Thank you, Captain." He turned to the nav-com officer, "Please acknowledge Obscure and follow USL15's directions for descent." Then he nodded to Cheral and turned his chair back to forward facing and lifted to the observation dome.

Cheral turned and headed back to the cadet's billeting compartments. They needed to change and be ready to launch once the transport was ready to unload.

◢

Q-STSX1, unveiled and with his bright red, flight

commander's diagonal double stripe highly visible, landed in the clearing with Obscure's closed launch bay portal abeam on his left. Kiile was directing the visible Peace Force Class XI transport into a hover over the portal and Q-KKLC14 with its bright red, single squadron stripe landed on STSX's right.

Stran and Casi had just stepped off the aft ramp, joined by Major Kooich and Leeana, when the transport's wide hangar bay and freight bay doors cracked open and slowly swung up.

'KIILE SAYS THEY ARE DISPATCHING THE PATROL FIGHTERS FIRST. HE HAS THEM ASSIGNED PARKING IMMEDIATELY TO OUR WEST. TTYF8 AND MKCC5 WILL LAND IMMEDIATELY TO OUR EAST.'

'Thanks STSX,' Casi said as she looked around and saw the two Q-Ships drifting into position. *'Are KVWC33 and LTVC21 on Patrol?'*

'YES. THEY ARE ESCORTING THE SPACE STATION AND MONITORING THE ORBITAL ALTITUDES FOR VISITORS. NO FOLLOWERS DETECTED.'

Casi was about to make a comment to STSX when the first patrol fighter emerged from the hangar bay's large opening. It moved toward them and the assigned landing spots, three others slowly drifted into view and followed it.

"They're just like the one you flew," Casi said, smiling at Stran, remembering the image he had shared at one time with her.

"Yes. I don't think the Force has changed anything about them since I was a cadet," he smiled back.

"Brings back memories, doesn't it," Major Kooich remarked in Stran's ear.

Almost in unison, the four fighters settled line abreast, facing Q-STSX1. Stran and Casi, with Major and Leeana Kooich, waited as the cadets conducted their post-flight checks and the canopies began to open one at a time. From the second fighter, Casi saw the pilot wave vigorously and pull her helmet off as she stood up.

Shara waved back as Cheral quickly descended the foot pockets and jumped to the ground, ignoring the last, extended steps. Cheral crossed the distance trying to maintain a semblance of formality and yet hurry. She stopped and quickly saluted the four of them.

The cadet's instructor pilot deplaned, along with the other two cadets, in time to see Cheral and Casi in a warm embrace. His expression turned rigid, his lips drawn tight as he led the other two cadets forward to meet the colonel.

He scowled at Cheral, obviously thinking her conduct inappropriate for a cadet as he brought them to 'Attention' and saluted.

"Colonel, Lieutenant," the instructor pilot said as they returned his salute. "My apologies, sir. I am Cadet Instructor Pilot, Captain Iims. May I present the cadet volunteers assigned to your campaign, Cadet Ani Tigs, Cadet Wilm Moss, and Captain Cheral Haak?" Again he looked sourly at Cheral and then back to the colonel. "I was not informed why you requested cadet volunteers, sir, but I must assume you have your reasons."

"Certainly," Stran said. "I always have my reasons."

Casi fought to hold her snicker and remained silent. She noticed that Cheral seemed unperturbed by the IP's manner and scowls.

"This is Lieutenant Casi Geaardt, my nav-com and a Q-Ship pilot," Stran said as Captain Iims noticed Casi's Space Pilot's ribbon, "and my wing commanders, Major Kooich and Lieutenant Leeana Kooich," Stran continued. "You will be seeing a lot of them while you are here." Then Stran stepped forward, past Captain Iims, and extended his forearm to the other two cadets. "Cadet Tigs, Cadet Moss. It is my personal pleasure to have you in this new training arena." Casi, Major Kooich and Leeana repeated Stran's greeting.

Then Stran smiled at Cheral. "It was a very pleasant surprise to see your name on the list of volunteers. Something to do with the director's challenge?"

"Sir?" Captain Iims asked. "Am I to understand you know Captain Haak?"

"Captain Iims," Stran continued and nodded to Cheral. "Captain Haak was my nav-com on STSX," he gestured to the Q-Ship behind him, "for three years before she requested flight training. Don't be concerned that Captain Haak will get preferential treatment while in training. All of the cadets will contend with my same, demanding expectations while training under my command."

"Yes, sir," Captain Iims stiffened. "I didn't mean to imply—"

"In public," Stran continued, "I will strive to address Captain Haak with the same decorum as any other cadet, but in informal company Commander Paal Haak's granddaughter and Lieutenant Geaardt's cousin will be addressed as family."

"Oh. Yes, sir," Captain Iims said. "I understand."

"When your cadets are not training or studying, or on mandatory rest," Stran continued, "they will report to Major Kooich for flight briefings and mission support as he feels necessary and appropriate. They are part of our fighter complement."

"But sir," Captain Iims rebutted. "They are just cadets."

"They are not 'just cadets' any longer, Captain," Stran said firmly. "They will train and they will fight as I need them. You will please expand their training to immediately include primary and advanced combat tactics and maneuvers. They will need it."

"Yes, sir," Captain Iims said, suddenly understanding more about the colonel's deeper intentions.

"If you will take Cadet Tigs and Cadet Moss through the hatchway to the left," Stran said pointing to the portal hatchway into the complex, "you will find Marine Seventeen inside ready to assist you with their billeting assignments. I believe the cadets will billet with the fighter crews. Captain Haak will join you in a few minutes."

"Yes, sir," Captain Iims said and turned toward the

hatchway with the two cadets in trail.

Cheral watched the trio leave and turned to Stran. "I see campaign commander suits you well."

"You do, do you?" He smiled at her. "Well Captain, you are officially requested to attend a dinner at the ranch this evening. Casual attire."

"Yes sir, but what have you done to STSX?" she asked, changing the subject and walking around STSX's left pylon and engine set to get a better look at the red stripes. "I couldn't believe my eyes when I saw him and KKLC14 as we departed the transport."

"Squadron colors," Major Kooich said with a proud air.

She noticed Casi's blush.

"Why bright red? Aren't Q-ships supposed to blend in when they aren't veiled?"

"He got the idea from the headbands Shara, Jill, and Rose wore in the attack on Ahaar's complex," Leeana explained.

"The red stands for the blood of my ancestors and others that have died or been stolen by the slavers," Casi admitted softly.

Cheral's eyes widened and her head nodded slowly as she studied the stripe.

"All of the ships will be similarly banded with a single stripe," Major Kooich said as he turned toward the hatchway, "including the patrol fighters. We are officially Able Squadron – Terra Campaign, but the colonel has nicknamed us the Apache Squadron," Major Kooich turned his head and winked at Casi, "after some half-blood he likes very much."

"Your headband, Captain," Leeana said, "will be waiting with your things in your apartment. All of us females have them."

"Let's go surprise Kiile," Stran said to Cheral. "I 'forgot' to tell him you were on the volunteer list and he'll need to bring you to dinner in a transport or on a remote."

⚔ ⚔ ⚔ ⚔ ⚔

Casi led Stran through STSX's aft portal and quickly climbed the ladder to the upper deck. She happily remembered Kiile's expression and huge smile when they led Cheral into the launch bay. Instructing the unloading crew as to where he wanted the various categories on the lading bill placed when they were brought inside, Kiile had just told a bay mechanic to open one quarter of the portal cover when he saw Stran and Casi patiently waiting for him to finish. He turned to speak to them when Cheral stepped from behind them and moved forward. Surprise was an understatement. It was the first time they had seen Kiile completely at a loss for words, and torn between his obvious feelings and his ingrained sense of protocol. To Casi's own surprise, she was pleased that he was able to maintain his poise and addressed Cheral properly as Captain. She knew a private reacquainting would happen as soon as they could arrange it.

She and Stran stayed long enough to meet the new flight mechanics, the second flight instructor and the numerous support personnel that arrived with the supplies and equipment. When the formalities were completed, Stran told her to take them back to the ranch.

Casi settled into the pilot's cushion chair and swiveled it to forward facing as Stran slipped into the jump seat to her right. STSX powered up and cloaked as they lifted through the shield barrier and into the clear air above the central valley. She turned STSX north and suddenly felt a new presence.

"There's a new ship descending from orbit," she said softly. "STSX, ask KVWC33 and LTVC21 if they have anything on it."

A moment passed, then STSX replied, "NEITHER HAVE ANY TARGETS. THEY HAVE BEEN PERIODICALLY BROADCASTING THE KNOWN CODES. NOTHING HAS APPEARED ON THE SCANNERS. ITS CLOAKING DOES NOT RESPOND TO THE CODES WE HAVE FILED.

THERE IS STILL NOTHING ON OUR VISUAL OR SENSOR SCANNERS."

"Thanks," Casi said. "I have a single coming from the northeast. Do you see it in my mind?"

"YES."

"STSX," Stran said as he watched Casi turn to intercept the target. "Contact KKLC14 and let the major know what's up."

"COMPLYING."

"Is there any way we can force it to land?" Casi asked Stran as she slowly lifted STSX's nose toward the descending ship.

"Nothing guaranteed," he said and thought a moment, "but it would be nice to see what cloaking it's using. I feel a crew of one."

"I agree," Casi said, "just one."

"STSX," Stran said quickly. "Ask Major Kooich to bring his two free Q-Ships and form up with us on the target. Give them the target's position off of Casi's sense."

Another moment passed. "KKLC14, TTYF8 and MKCC5 will be airborne in less than three minutes."

Casi smiled at Stran and then focused on the target's feeling. "Maybe we can make him think his cloaking has failed."

"That's what I'm thinking, Bren."

⚔

It was less than the three minutes when KKLC14, TTYF8 and MKCC5 joined up with the false scanner position that STSX displayed for them.

"It's your show Colonel," Major Kooich's voice said, softly filling STSX's cockpit. "Where do you want us?"

"We'll drop in low and behind him about fifty yards," Stran said. "Put one of you on each side of him at about the same distance and one of you should settle in front of him. When you're all in position, I'll give him a hail and see if we can convince him to land."

In seconds, the four Q-Ships surrounded the unsuspecting

target and Casi remarked, "It's definitely a fighter, single place, about the size of a short range patrol fighter."

"Keep your shields up," Stran said and STSX relayed the command and opened the multichannel hailing frequencies and set the transmit power to close range.

Stran alerted the target. "To the unidentified fighter in terran airspace over the pine valley, hold your present course and do not deviate. You have four heavy fighters in formation. Any attempt to deviate and you will be fired upon."

The ship oscillated slightly and Casi attributed it to his surprise at the hail.

"All ships, drop visual cloaking. Visual only," Stran ordered and the four Q-ships suddenly coalesced.

The still invisible fighter moved up, thinking it could escape vertically, but all four Q-Ships crisscrossed cannon shots over it. The fighter stopped and darted downward; crisscrossing cannon shots beneath it changed his mind and he slowly settled back in between the Q-Ships.

"Stay focused, love," Stran said softly. "I think he's nibbling." Then to the unidentified fighter, he continued, "Stay in position and follow your leader to a landing. Any deviations or aggression and you will be fired upon, likely destroyed."

Slowly KKLC14 steepened the descent and Casi recognized the clearing about five miles below Obscure. They had destroyed a transport there once, deploying a dozen ground soldiers sent to spy on and collect intelligence information about Obscure.

"STSX," Stran continued, "tell Kiile and KKLC14 that I want all four of the patrol fighters and some of his marines down here 'On the Double!' I think we have a present for him. Have the patrol fighters arrive visually unveiled and sensor blocked. Have them report to KKLC14."

When KKLC14 had given Kiile time to respond, he slowed above the clearing, Stran told the Q-Ships to hover and then he hailed the fighter again and demanded that it descend to a landing, reminding it that an attempt to escape would end his career suddenly.

Kiile's men surrounded the landing site and the four patrol fighters took quartering positions between each of the Q-Ships. The interloper took the hint and settled into the clearing, but when it did nothing more, Stran hailed the ship and ordered it to completely power down and for the pilot to exit the ship.

"All Q-Ships," Stran said. "Two cannon shots each, on your sides. Two in front, two behind and two on either side. Close but no hits please."

Dirt and valley floor debris suddenly filled the area around the still invisible ship, confirming to the pilot that the Q-Ships knew exactly where he was. In seconds, the fighter coalesced in the center of the clearing and the canopy slowly swung open. Kiile's Marines, weapons ready, quickly surrounded the pilot as he looked up and acknowledged the eight ships poised and ready, encircling his position.

"We've got him, Colonel," Kiile said to the Q-Ships. "Do you want us to bring his ship in?"

"Yes," Stran admitted. "We'll meet you back at the facility." Then he said, "Major Kooich, 'Well done.' Please pass a 'Well done' and my 'Thanks' to each of your crews."

Then he turned to look at Casi. "And a very 'Well done' to you Bren. We couldn't have done this without you and your abilities. You never cease to amaze me."

She smiled. "Thanks, love."

Marshal Wally Lima was making his afternoon rounds when Kenny called on the short range communicator in Wally's jeep.

"Marshal," Kenny's voice said. "I have a message from Hank at the Smallwood ranch. He says someone named Greg from the ranch needs to meet and talk to you. Are you available?"

Wally smiled and said, "Yes. Does he have a preference of where to meet?"

"He asked that you stop by Rose Mitchell's place," Kenny replied. "In about twenty minutes."

"I can make that," Wally said. "Is he still on the line?"

"Yes."

"Tell him I'll be there."

Wally finished his drive around the college and worked his way south and around the high school complex once, then turned toward the south bridge and Rose's place. At first he did not see anyone as he pulled into the snow packed drive and stopped in front of the wide veranda, but as he got out, Greg, Shara and Rose came out of the front door and motioned him in.

"Too cold to just stand around," Rose said as she closed the door behind them.

"Thanks for coming, Wally," Greg said and extended his hand.

Wally returned the gesture, and then shook Shara and Rose's hands. "Kenny sounded like something's up."

"Nothing urgent," Greg said, "except that I have a present from the director for you."

"Really?" Wally asked, skeptical. "From the director?"

"Yes," Greg said and gestured to the chairs around Rose's dining room table as he seated Shara and then himself. "A remote for the Riggin Marshal's specific use."

"A remote? Like your number Five?"

"Very similar," Shara added. "Just a bit less firepower."

Wally just shook his head. "So what's the catch?"

"Wally," Greg started slowly. "You need surveillance capabilities that you can control and communicate with. We'll keep Five linked so we can have a fast warning if you need our help. The remote the director sent will accept commands from you and from us. You will be expected to use it for your investigations and intelligence gathering, as well as personal protection.

"Also, the three new deputies that are assigned to you were handpicked and each has a GPF tag. They can be trusted to help you in this duality, and the remote will help you keep watch over them and to aide them if they run into trouble." Greg opened a small carrysack and handed Wally four small earpieces. "These are small enough that few will notice them, and those that do will rightly suspect they are communication devices for you and the deputies. But they won't realize that all four of you will communicate through and with the remote."

"Wow. Can the deputies tell it what to do?" Wally asked.

"Only to the extent that you allow" Shara added. "The new remote will operate in cloaked mode unless you specifically tell it to unveil. I wouldn't do that unless it's absolutely necessary."

"How will I know where it is," Wally asked, confused, "if I can't see it?"

"It'll always tell you where it is," Shara continued with Greg's nod. "After a very short time, you'll just know, sort of a feeling."

"Through your remote," Greg said, "you'll also be able to communicate with us, through a remote to remote link. Five always keeps us up to date and it will let us know when you ask for us or for something from us. Like Five, your new remote can record and relay conversations, even those inside a dwelling or building, record or relay images, real-time or archived."

"How do I see the images it records?" Wally asked.

Greg pointed to a small box on Rose's bar top counter. "There are four image displays in that box. They are portable and rechargeable. Carry them or keep them in your office. Your choice."

"We'll have one of Kiile's Marines set up the remote's charging station tomorrow," Shara said. "Probably best if it's at your house, somewhere it won't be noticed. He can also stop by your office and install the display's rechargers."

Rose stepped up and set three auto-chill steins on the table. Wally looked up, startled. He had not realized she had left the table to get them.

"You look like you could use one of these, Wally," Rose said with a smile. "We won't tell anyone you did."

He smiled at her. "I'm that bad, huh?"

"Yeah," Shara said and pushed one to him and took one herself. Rose took the third and Wally looked at Greg with a question.

"I'll get something later Wally," Greg said and leaned back in his chair. "When you're done, we'll take you out back to meet Wally Lima's remote number One, WL-One for short."

▲ ▲ ▲ ▲ ▲

Greg and Shara relaxed in the casual portion of the main house's living room, Greg in the overstuffed chair near the fireplace and Shara crosswise on his lap facing the room. They were quietly recounting the day's accomplishments when Matti led Jim Woods, Bill Woods and Gary Woods through the dining room from the back door.

Greg greeted them without rising and Shara waved.

"I wasn't expecting a dinner invite," Jim said. "Something going on?"

"Does something always have to be going on?" Shara asked.

"With you two," he smiled back, "it's most likely."

"Our new cadets and supplies came today," Greg said, as Matti opened the back door again.

Matti squealed and there was a little commotion at the door before Matti happily ushered Cheral into the living room, Kiile trailing behind her.

"Obviously Matti," Kiile said softly, "you are happier to see Cheral than me."

She turned and shook her finger at him. "We're always happy to see you Mr. Kiile, but seeing Miss Cheral is a very big and happy surprise." Then she winked at him, "And you know it, too!"

"Yes, Matti," Kiile admitted. "I felt exactly the same way when she showed up unexpectedly."

"Anyways, Miss Cheral wouldn't like you going around hugging women you just happen to meet," Matti added and then turned to Greg. "Mr. Greg, are more coming? Besides our regular four?"

"Just Paul, Matti," he answered and nodded.

At his gesture, Matti quickly turned to each and asked if they had a drink preference, and when she had taken their orders, she hurried back to the kitchen.

Cheral said her 'hellos' to Jim, Bill and Gary and had just settled on the long couch with Kiile when Jill led Nick in the back door, followed by Major Kooich and Leeana.

"Cheral?" Jill half shouted in surprised question. "You're back?" Jill darted across the living room and hugged Cheral's shoulders before she got up.

"Yes Jill," Cheral finally said. "I was happy to come until I heard the colonel's conversation with our IP."

Jill and Nick took the love seat across from Cheral and Kiile and Jill asked what she meant. "What's an IP?"

"Instructor Pilot, Jill. Colonel?" Cheral asked when Jill questioned her. "Were you serious when you said the cadets are part of Major Kooich's fighter wing?"

"Definitely," Greg said in answer. "You and the other cadets are going to learn to fight and survive and not just run through exercises. Remember the director's challenge at the party? I don't know how much combat experience you'll see here in terran space, but like you saw today, there will be encounters and you will be part of the defenses and the offenses when you're not training."

"Like they saw today?" Jill asked. "Suddenly I feel like I'm out of the loop."

"We were on the ground about two hours," Cheral explained, "when Kiile got a call from the colonel and Shara. They needed fighter support to help contain an unidentified fighter and Kiile's marines to collect its pilot. The cadets reported to Major Kooich in flight and Kiile and his men encircled the landing site. Kiile said we couldn't light the target up, so I was surprised the fighter showed on our scanners."

Greg was about to continue when Matti and Cara returned and served the drink orders. He waited until everyone had their drinks and then continued. "STSX sent out a false scanner target based on Shara's sense of where it was. It was a gamble that the pilot would think his cloaking had failed. He apparently did, which let us convince him he should land and save his hide." Then he turned serious, "Back to your question, Cheral, I am implementing a few changes in the way we train for this campaign. Most of it will be practicing the teachings in actual combat. Everyone will learn. And quickly!"

"That's how I learned," Shara admitted softly.

Matti hurried through the dining room and led Paul in. She took his drink order and hurried back to the kitchen as Paul greeted everyone, especially Cheral. "I hear you cadets have already been exposed to real combat."

Cheral smiled. "You forget I've seen real combat before," she patted her chest, "but I agree today was different."

"Kiile," Greg said, "did the technicians find out anything about the fighter?"

"Some," Kiile admitted, "though not as much as we hoped for. They're still working on it and will eventually make it give up its secrets."

"Did you get the director's 'special' package he sent to you?" Greg asked.

"The body cloaking transmitters?" He saw Greg nod. "Yes, I certainly did. They're a very nice addition to our equipment."

Greg nodded again. "I knew you had never asked for any and after your difficulties at Ahaar's complex, I decided they would be useful." Then he took a folded envelope out of his shirt pocket and passed it to Cheral and asked her to pass it down to Jim.

"One reason I asked you tonight Jim," Greg said, "is that I received this from the director. It was delivered by the transport captain that arrived today.

Jim took the envelope, removed the letter and began reading the content. Slowly his expression broadened into a smile.

"You should receive official notification," Greg added, "within a day or two through your office in Lynchburg."

"What is it Jim?" Bill asked, roused by his son's expression and Greg's words.

"This says I'm being promoted to Captain," Jim said softly and looked up at Greg's wide smile.

Greg raised his cup of coffee and gestured around the room. "Congratulations, Captain Woods. Thank you for your unwavering support, determination and resourcefulness. You deserve this."

Everyone joined Greg in his toast and when the cheering finally settled, Matti entered the living room and stopped in front of Paul.

"Sorry to be late with your drink," she apologized and when he said it was all right, she turned to Greg and Shara. "Mrs. Shara, dinner is ready to be served."

"Thank you Matti," Shara said and got up and gestured everyone into the dining room.

Eighty

Wednesday, December 13

Jill sat on the edge of her bed in Shara's guest room and pondered the director's offer and the lengthy discussion she and Nick had with Shara and Greg. She was encouraged by Major Kooich and Leeana's presence in the meeting, even though they did not actually add anything to the conversation. She felt they were strongly in agreement with them becoming part of what Greg had called their 'personal protection team.'

She had gone over so much in her mind since that discussion, wondering if she was actually ready to make the leap now that the precipice was in front of her. She told them that she was, and now she had the worst case of butterflies she had ever had. Not accustomed to making decisions of this magnitude, she remembered how quickly she defended herself and Greg on the emissary's frigate, how simple it was for her when she reacted and stopped the trooper trying to kill Shara in Obscure's mines, how easy it was to accept and move forward when she and Shara went to find Nick in a blizzard on the reservation, how confident she was when they confronted Louis before he could attack Kiile, how right it was when they confronted and captured old Judge Bernice right out there on the front drive, how angry she felt when she thought Harry had killed Shara and how determined she was to eradicate him for his deed.

All of this made her realize how much she cared about Shara. Shara had been her only best friend since before high school and had shared in nearly every joy and heartache she had had over the years. And now, Shara was giving her something else to share, something so monumental she could barely get her arms around it. And Shara had taken her case all the way to the director of the Peace Force himself!

Her thoughts had wavered back and forth until she remembered how thrilled she had been when she realized she also shared the hidden family talent, the never-talked-about capability of silently talking to others, to Shara and to Greg. She had accused Shara of pulling her leg when Shara had disclosed that she had the capability, but understood beyond words when the talent finally awoke within her and she heard Greg chiding her! How wonderfully startled she had been! She had never before felt such a sense of belonging, not even while she was growing up with her father and mother.

Yes, Jill decided, *this is what I'm meant to do. To not move forward would be a terrible misuse of the talent of my ancestors, and the trust and confidence that everyone around Greg and Shara have given me,*

Jill pushed herself up off the bed and double checked her clothing. Before the day that she and Shara had spied on the Trader's meeting and had gotten caught, she had always adhered to her mother's demands for prim and proper dress with nothing out of place, wrinkled or soiled, women in dresses and men in pants. She looked at herself in the mirror, at the changed self she saw. That day and every day since, she had taken on Shara's casual, confident look of jeans and a blouse, sometimes sparkling and pressed and sometimes rumpled and smudged. Today was in between, clean but not actually pressed jeans and a pretty green blouse over her Blues. She double checked the back of her wide, western belt to be sure the cloaking transmitter was not visible and she patted the Kaaspr in her front pocket, the same place where Shara told her she always kept hers.

Satisfied, she picked up her heavy coat and walked to the dining room, expecting to see Greg and Shara like they usually were, sitting in the overstuffed chair by the fire. But they were not there and she turned to the back door and called Three.

'Greg,' she said in her mind, *'I'm off to talk with father at the mill. I'm taking Three. Wish me luck.'*

'Shara is waiting on Seven,' Greg's voice replied.

'I'm going to escort you in and wait for you, Jill,' Shara's voice added. *'I'm not comfortable with either of us going into town alone. Not yet.'*

'Thanks, Shar,' Jill said, knowing her relief was showing in her tone as she stepped out onto the back porch and saw Shara waiting, hovering just beyond the steps into the yard.

"Do you have everything?" Shara asked as Jill mounted Three's stirrup.

"I think so. A remote, a cloaking transmitter, one Kaaspr and me," she said, patting her front pocket, "and you, my escort."

"Then let's do it," Shara said and swung Seven away from the porch to make room as Three rose up and led the way over the trees.

▲

Fully cloaked, Jill led them to the west end of the mill's long main office building and settled next to the steps leading up to the single, centered door. Shara felt the building and the buildings around them.

'No one's outside,' Shara said as she stepped off of Seven. *'There are a few in the shipping building just north of us.'*

'I think I feel them,' Jill said, surprised by the faint sensation.

'Good. Your father's alone in his office,' Shara continued. *'The remotes will watch the entrances and I'll be here.'*

Jill stepped up on the first step, mentally toggled her veil off and hurried into the long hallway inside. She stopped at the third office and peeked through the open door.

"You up to a visitor?" she asked as her father looked up from the papers on his desk. Jill noticed and pointed to the stack, "Still no computers for all of that?"

"Good morning, Jill," he said happily hurrying around the desk to hug her. "How's my absentee daughter doing? I haven't seen you in a few days. When was it? Friday?" He absently pushed the door behind her and it partially closed.

"Probably," Jill said as he gestured to a chair facing the corner of his desk, its back slightly turned toward the door.

"So. You said you need to discuss plans for your future," Jack said as he settled into his chair and set the stack of papers aside.

"Yes. Can we talk here?" she asked.

"Sure," he said. "No one here but us regulars."

"Okay," she said and started explaining the discussion she and Nick had with Greg and Shara and the Peace Force director's offer.

They discussed the pros and cons, her financial status and the requirements of her trust and how all of this might be affected by her and Nick's recently announced intentions to marry in the spring. They were just putting the finishing thoughts on a plan when Jill heard Shara's urgent call, the hair stood up on the back of her neck and the office door burst open.

She shoved herself back and jumped up in a turn, placing herself between Jack and the doorway. She had her Kaaspr out just as the first bolt hit her and threw her backwards across Jack's desk. She barely felt the second bolt as it hit her side and caught Jack's arm. She heard someone yell her name as everything went black.

⚜

For no particular reason, Lou looked out of the shipping office's single south facing window as he filed the folders from the morning's transfers. He didn't hear any voices or the crunching of snow, but something caught his attention and he stopped and watched the west end of the main office building, situated a little to the east. He noticed a faint shimmer and startled, saw Jill Thomas suddenly appear out of thin air and slip inside through the door.

He closed his open mouth and tried to grasp her sudden appearance. Then he remembered Judge Bernice Reeds said she had been shipped off to some prince somewhere for a payment the Family owed, and now? There she was, though the image was fleeting. But he knew he had seen her. *How could I mistake her for anyone else? I've worked in shipping for twenty years, and I've seen her growing up, visiting and when she started college and began working here at the mill. That was three years ago. Her height, her red hair, even in her heavy coat, I could not be mistaken.*

Lou turned to his desk, sat down and thought about what this meant, why she might be here. *She must be here to see her dad, but why? Is she trying to get her old job back? No, that does not make sense. No one has even seen her around town since...* His mind reeled as he realized no one had seen her since the night of the Trader's meeting, the 15th of October. *Where has she been for two months?*

Lou took a box from the bottom desk drawer on the right and unlocked it. He unwrapped the Greymn hand laser and slipped it into his pocket as he dropped the box back into the drawer. *I wonder if she knows anything about the judge's or Harry Woods' disappearances?*

He slipped his coat on and picked up a few folders from his desk, turned to the door and walked into the sorting room. At the east end of the shipping and receiving building, he stepped out into the cold and crossed to the main office building.

He casually greeted Alice and turned down the hall toward Jack's office. As he got closer, he could hear her talking. Jill and her dad were discussing training and finances and—

Suddenly, he felt someone was watching and that he had to act quickly! He pulled the Greymn from his pocket and shoved the door open.

⋀

Shara felt Lou in the shipping office, but did not pay him any attention until she felt the change in his aura as he sat down at his desk and opened a desk drawer. She focused on his activity as he got up, walked the length of the shipping and receiving building and crossed to the main offices. He stopped beside Jack's office door, but she had barely alerted Jill that he was listening when Shara felt him draw the Greymn.

Shara shoved the door open and burst in just as the Greymn fired. Lou turned at the sound of the door and fired a second shot into the office as Shara simultaneously unveiled and fired the single optic, Brekshiir 170 on her left wrist and the Kaaspr in her right hand.

Shara's mind shrieked Jill's name as her momentum carried her to the open doorway and Lou's lifeless body toppled sideways and sprawled on the floor.

▲ ▲ ▲ ▲ ▲

Wally was sitting at his desk, idly toying with one of the three earpieces he had in front of him when his three deputies came in from the front parking lot.

"Sorry we're running late, Marshal," Thom said as he pulled the chair from behind his desk and settled to one side of Wally's. "Dan had to make a call so we decided to wait for him. Hope that was okay."

"Sure Thom," Wally said and gestured for the others to settle nearby. "And it's Wally. Save the Marshal bit until I'm mad or we're in public." Wally leaned back in his chair and waited as they settled. Then he asked, "How're the temporary accommodations working out?"

Ted smiled. "Better for me than for the college kids in the next apartment," he said with a broad smile. "The last thing they expected was to have a deputy for a neighbor."

Dan indicated his was okay, and Thom said it'd do until they could get a real place and get settled properly.

"Well, Bill thinks he may have places by the end of the week," Wally said with a smile. "I'm not sure what he has in mind, but he'll treat you right."

Wally leaned forward and picked up an earpiece. He held it in his hand and slowly turned it in his fingers. "Yesterday, I had a meeting with a friend of mine. An old friend I should say and he told me you each have a Peace Force tag." He watched their expressions go from start to slow smiles. "I have one also, but I can't sense others yet."

"And your friend?" Thom asked.

"Yes, he has one too. Since I got here in Riggin, my friend has been watching out for me," Wally admitted, "though I didn't realize it. I had been here a month before I found out he was here and what he was doing." He continued to watch the earpiece as he turned it. "He had set a cloaked remote to tail me everywhere I went and that remote and his connections saved my hide on at least one occasion that I can think of."

"Remotes? Here?" Ted asked, disbelieving Wally's claim. "I haven't ever seen one, but I've heard about them."

"Well, I'm going to do you one better than that," Wally said and smiled at each of them. "The Peace Force director—"

"The director?" Dan interrupted.

"Yes, the director," Wally confirmed. "He's watching the situation here and my friend's handling of things very closely."

"So this whole missing person's thing is much bigger than you let on initially," Thom said.

"Yes it is. And our part is also much bigger."

Wally handed Thom the earpiece he was toying with and then handed the two others to Dan and Ted.

"My friend gave me a gift from the director, our own remote." Wally waited until their expressions steadied again. "These earpieces," he tapped the one he was wearing, "will provide us four with direct communications at any time while we're wearing them, through the remote. My friend is also keeping his remote linked to ours and in some cases it will follow us to be available if we need it."

"I noticed there's no radio reception around here," Dan said, puzzled. "Just short range stuff."

"Something about the makeup of the valley, I'm told," Wally agreed. "The remote will overcome that limitation."

Wally went on to explain the details of the remote's operation and how he saw it fitting into their daily rounds and situational awareness. When he got to the image storage and play back capabilities, he pulled a box from under his desk and passed a small image display to each of them.

"Each of your desks has been wired so that you can set the displays beside your monitors, like this," Wally said as he placed his display to the right side of his desk monitor. "They will recharge if they are placed here within about an eight inch circle. And I'm told a charge will last about three days if you use them remotely."

Wally explained how they should communicate with the remote, how to get voice and image replays or downloads, and how to get it to follow when they felt they needed additional backup.

"Oh, and it's armed with two laser weapons," Wally said as the phone console chimed. "Excuse me a sec," he said and picked up the hand unit.

His expression went blank and he listened intently and then hung up.

"That was Gary Woods up at the mill," he said. "Thom, I need you to come with me, and you, Ted and Dan, need to make our mid-morning rounds."

"Sure," Thom said as Ted and Dan nodded and headed out to their patrol cars.

"Get your patrol car and meet me at the mill," Wally said.

Thom locked the front office door as he went out and Wally tapped his earpiece and said, "WL-One, follow me," as he locked the back door and went to his jeep.

'Jill, wake up,' Greg's voice said to her confused mind.

'Jill! It's Shar. Wake up.'

Suddenly the strong smell of ammonia pierced her senses and Jill coughed. She coughed again as she tried to open her eyes.

"Damn!" she said softly, feeling the intense pain in her chest and side as the coughing made her body bend, her muscles contract. "Damn, that hurts!"

Jill forced her eyes open and saw Greg's face, close, staring back at her.

"Good to see you awake," he said with a wide smile.

Suddenly the memory snapped back and Jill tried to jerk free and twist to see where her father was.

"Hold still," Greg demanded. "He's all right. He's in Medical on STSX."

"What..." she mumbled, trying to understand. "You're here? Already?"

"Yes," Shara said softly. "You've been unconscious for a little while."

Jill tried to compose herself, but Greg did not release her and Shara did not move away. She could not move if she wanted to.

"Who?" she finally asked. "Who was it?"

"Lou from shipping," Greg said.

Gary Woods' head came into view as he leaned closer for Jill to see. "Doug suspected Lou when we talked over a month ago. But I thought I could watch him and intervene if he tried anything. I'm very sorry Jill. I had no idea he would try to kill someone, much less try to kill you."

"Who could've guessed?" she said and slowly tried to sit up. "Help me up, please. You shouldn't be holding me."

Greg slowly leaned her upright and said, "You're my little sister and I'll hold you if I want to, so stop complaining. Now slowly."

Shara stepped in front of her and helped Greg lift her to her feet. She wobbled a little, but was able to stand, holding onto Greg. Shara caught her chin and turned her face from side to side. "Looks like you got a little flash burn," she said as she

81

glanced at Greg. "Medical can fix that while it checks you out."

"Man, I hurt all over," she said with a tight smile. "Front, back, sides." She turned to look at the desk, between her and the door. "Wasn't I over there?" She pointed to the doorway and the upturned chair.

"You were thrown into and over the desk," Shara said, "but you kept your dad safe. He only got hit in the arm." Shara handed her the Kaaspr she retrieved from the floor. "Here, put this back in your pocket."

Jill looked down at her shredded blouse and her exposed body suit. "Good thing I wore my Blues," she giggled and coughed at the stab of pain. "This might be embarrassing if I hadn't."

Shara smiled at Greg as he started moving Jill toward the door. "Major Kooich has moved Lou's body and has just finished 'visiting' the folks here in the offices. Time for us to go."

C.3482.367

Merchandise Director Korveel entered Chairman Sorgat's office, walked around the long conference table and approached his wide, oval desk.

"Director Korveel," the chairman said as he paused the display on the monitor hovering above his desk. "Thank you for coming."

"Chairman Sorgat," he said as he stopped beside the desk, ignoring the data he could see through the monitor's transparent screen. "I just heard there was another Intelligence drop near the terran launch site, Point Obscure."

The chairman nodded, "I too found out this morning. I contacted one of the intelligence directors on a different matter and in the conversation he asked if I knew anything about defenses at Point Obscure. What they might be."

Director Korveel waited. He had no knowledge of any

defenses.

"I told the intelligence director that Point Obscure did not have any physical defenses. It was secured by our troopers and sophisticated cloaking." The chairman got up from his chair and began to pace slowly behind it. "'Why was he concerned about defenses?' I asked the director," the Chairman continued as he rubbed his chin. "He told me they had decided to investigate themselves since so many other attempts had failed. He felt they were better suited to investigate without being seen than the others that had been sent." The chairman looked at Director Korveel and shrugged.

"They thought they could succeed when others, even military troopers, had failed?"

The chairman nodded. "It seems Intelligence lost contact with the transport and the agents early in the third turn after they were inserted."

"I can see," Korveel said with a nod, "why Intelligence asked the question."

The chairman started pacing again. "It seems I am not any better than Director Ahaar was or than Intelligence was."

"Sir?"

"I asked for the help of the prince in the loan of a reconnaissance ship and a single pilot to fly a low risk mission for me. A simple sensor scan of the area to see what could be detected," the chairman said and looked at the director through the haze of the idle screen. "I did not heed my own advice and now I fear I have lost the prince's ship and his pilot."

"Lost? You did not send them to check on Point Obscure?"

The chairman nodded slowly. "No response in thirty pars. The black hole called Obscure has devoured them as well as all of the ones before them. Intelligence suspects the Peace Force Shadows may be monitoring and defending that area."

The director reached for the back of a nearby chair and steadied himself. "I assume the prince does not yet know."

"That would be a correct assumption." The chairman

resumed his pacing. "Have you had any luck contacting the new terran facility?"

"Yes, some," Director Korveel said.

The chairman stopped and looked at him.

"They are without fighters and without transports," Director Korveel said. "They do not have the seed families they were promised and are thus without the manpower to continue the construction. Without transports, they cannot receive supplies necessary to continue. They ask if we are prepared to provide what they need?"

"Can they confirm or deny what we think happened to Director Ahaar?" the Chairman asked, ignoring the question.

"No. Only that all communications and protection and the last of the supplies ceased approximately fourteen turns past." Director Korveel cleared his throat and glanced away before continuing. "Given the recent events and your understanding of what Intelligence thinks, this is possibly not the best suggestion, but I think we should send two transports with supplies and workers to bolster the work effort on the new launch facility."

"What?" the Chairman said, his voice shrill with disbelief. "Send more?"

"Provide fighter escorts, but stay completely away from Point Obscure's coordinates," director Korveel said calmly. "Let the fighters protect the transports, and take the transports directly to the new launch facility. It is on the opposite side of the globe from Point Obscure."

The chairman thought about the director's proposal. "Do you think you can get two transports down to the surface without being intercepted, or being detected?"

"I can only hope," Director Korveel said. "If we do not go near Point Obscure, I feel we may not alert whoever is watching and protecting that area. Possibly, they could send a fighter up and rendezvous with the freighters instead?"

"I will see what I can do," Chairman Sorgat said with a sigh.

"We do have to try something. We need that facility and the perishables they ship."

⊼ ⊼ ⊼ ⊼ ⊼

Nick parked his truck beside the bunkhouse garage and went into the main house looking for Jill, Shara or Greg. When he did not find Jill in the house or her room, he slipped into the kitchen and found Cara and Annie.

"Where is everybody?" he asked as he looked at one and then the other.

"Mr. Nick," Cara said slowly. "Miss Jill is out in Mrs. Shara's ship, her and her dad."

"Did something happened?" he asked as he turned to the door.

"I don't know what for sure," Cara said, "but there was a problem when Miss Jill went to the mill."

Nick hurried, shoved the kitchen door open and dashed through the dining room and out onto the back porch. He saw STSX in his usual place and hurried for the aft portal.

The panels cycled open and then closed as Nick dove through into the central aisle. He saw Shara and Greg sitting in one double wide seat on the right, and stopped in front of them.

"What happened? Where's Jill?' he said in a rush. "Cara said—"

"In here," Shara said as she got up and led him to the left side Medical couch. "She's fine, just flash burns from Lou's Greymn and some bruising. You'll have to be gentle when you hold her."

"Is she all right? Can I talk to her? Can I—" The questions started spilling out of him.

"Easy Nick," Greg said as he grasped his shoulder and nodded to Shara. "Medical has kept her asleep since we got her on board. Better for healing."

With Shara's touch on the keypad, the clear cover unsealed and slowly rolled back. Nick was instantly on his knees beside the couch and took Jill's hand.

"What happened?" he finally asked, his voice more controlled.

Shara quietly explained the morning's happenings and how Jill had protected her father in the surprise attack. She kept telling him that Jill was all right and Medical said her burns were superficial and would heal completely.

Slowly Nick listened and absorbed what Shara was saying. Still holding Jill's hand, he turned and looked at the other Medical couch.

"And Jack?" he asked softly.

"He'll be up for a little bit tonight," Greg said. "Jill deflected Lou's second shot, but it got Jack's right arm. He's mending very well and by morning he'll be fine."

Nick nodded and turned back to Jill as she slowly began to move. She rolled her head toward them and he watched as she opened her eyes.

"Nick?" she asked, still confused.

"I'm here," he answered and leaned up and kissed her.

▲ ▲ ▲ ▲ ▲

Shara lay awake long after everyone had either gone or turned in for the night, cuddled as close to Greg as she could. She rested her head on his arm with her forehead gently against his chest, his free arm curled possessively around her, holding her close under the soft fleece sheets and the warm bed quilt. She could feel his mind working and his soft breathing belied the outward peacefulness of their sanctuary.

"Greg?" she asked softly.

"Yeah?" His clear response confirmed what she already knew.

"Do you think today may have changed Jill's decision?" she asked the most obvious question.

"I'll be surprised if it did," he said softly. "She was determined before you two went to see Jack, and her reflexes were sound when Lou attacked. She instinctively moved to protect him and she had her Kaaspr almost out before he fired, fully intent on defending herself."

"But her response could have been simply a reflex."

"I don't think so. Not that way, Bren," he said and held her a little tighter. "Jill suffered almost as much as you did at the hands of the Family. She hasn't turned from a fight since we rescued her. I think her mind is made up."

"I hope so," she admitted.

Greg chuckled to himself. "Jack told me tonight that Jill had tried to explain to him why she hadn't gone back and picked up her studies and that he'd just passed it off thinking she just didn't like her classes. But he admitted that today he finally got it. He sees why she can't just go back. He also thinks her mind is made up and he wants to work out a new arrangement for her trust fund."

"I'm glad he sees the dilemma she's facing," Shara said, then returned to their original thoughts. "I think Nick is pretty determined as well."

"He might not be if Jill wasn't involved," Greg said, "but under the circumstances, I think he's in. We'll confirm their positions in the morning."

"Rose was thrilled. She already told me so," Shara said and slipped her arm under his waist. "Before we went after Ahaar, she was upset that there wasn't enough time to train better."

"I think Doug's the only question," he said. "He's been training with Rose and I'm hoping he'll continue when Rose tells him she's in."

Shara thought to herself for a long moment. "If it comes to a fight, where will you use the four of them? I mean, a lot of the fighting is likely to be ship against ship, not normal Shadow work."

"But I still need Shadows," he said and kissed the top of her head. "We still have a valley full of Reeds to either convert or to monitor. We still have to find that second launch facility and we have to collect intelligence on their progress and activities."

Shara tipped her head back to look at him in the dim light of the bedroom. "You mean send them out in the field to do reconnaissance work?"

"Maybe," he said with a weak smile. "If I did, they'd have to have a few of Kiile's marines to help them, someone with more experience."

"That's a relief," she said with a sigh. "For a minute I thought you were going to just throw them in the pond and see if they can swim."

"Even with help," he said soberly, "it'll be a lot like that. But initially, we'll use them close at hand, where they can learn to protect themselves and the rest of us."

Again, Shara considered his words for a long moment before she changed the subject.

"Did I tell you that Jim asked if we could take him back to Lynchburg?" she asked. "He also wants to bring Shelly and Carrie Anne back next week."

"Either of us can take him back," Greg said, "and bring them back out. When does he need to be back?"

"Sometime tomorrow."

"Okay. Why don't you take him once Jack is out of Medical. I need to sit with Hench and Kiile and do a little planning."

"Do you realize we're half way through the holiday season," she asked, "and we haven't even thought about planning a gathering? At least, thanks to the girls and Hank, we have a decently decorated house for it. I know Jim wants Shelly and Carrie Anne to be here with their families for the holidays."

Greg did not say anything.

"You do want to have your mother and Brendan here, don't you?" She waited looking at him.

"Yes," he finally said. "It's just... that I don't remember ever decorating or celebrating the holidays."

"What?" She raised up on an elbow. "Never?"

"If we ever did, it was before mother's mate, Tom, was killed and she went missing."

Shara settled back down beside him and curled her arms around him. "Well then, I think you need to tell your mother that they are expected to come for the holidays. We'll pick them up whenever you arrange it and I'll organize the house girls and the hands to get the place ready. Oh, and you'll have to arrange your campaign schedule around our first Christmas together."

"Okay," he laughed softly. "I'll see what I can do."

Shara kissed him fully as she stretched her length against him. He stroked her back softly and held her tight in response.

Eighty-One
Thursday, December 15

Wally glanced at the clock beside the marshal's office front door and realized he was cutting it close. He switched his network monitor off and placed his open paperwork in a desk drawer and locked it. Ted was finishing the late rounds and everything seemed to be quiet enough. Dan went off duty at seven and Kenny had enjoyed a day without any demands on his time. Thom would come on at two and relieve Ted.

Wally tapped his earpiece and said, "Ted, I'm locking up the office. If you need me, you know where I'll be." Stepping out onto the lighted stoop, he locked the backdoor behind him. Wally drove down Baxter and turned in the alley behind Hap's, stopping in the back parking lot beside Carole's jeep just as she stepped out of the back door.

"Hey, stranger," she said with a broad smile and stopped beside his open window. "When I didn't see you for lunch or dinner, I wondered if I would tonight."

"Sorry I missed seeing you today, but things were a little busy," he said.

"Did you get a chance to stop at Jerry's, or Connie's or somewhere?" she asked and leaned in and kissed him.

"Not yet," he admitted sheepishly.

"Honestly, Wally, having the deputies is no help if you still work yourself to death." Carole stared at him as she straightened up. "Come on, follow me home and we'll see what we can find."

⋏

Wally parked in the drive and followed Carole into the house through the garage. Carole keyed the garage door closed and led the way in.

He took her coat and hung it on a peg behind the front door. As he hung his coat on an adjacent peg, he realized they were becoming very comfortable with each other's company. He was very pleased that Carole spoke freely about how she felt and what she thought. He liked that she looked forward to seeing him, and he smiled to himself and admitted that he felt the same way about her.

Carole had kicked her shoes off by the door like she always seemed to do, but then she went straight to the kitchen and began searching the refrigerator and a nearby cabinet.

"How about left over seasoned chicken on fettuccini with Alfredo sauce?" she asked and turned to get his answer. "I can throw together a salad to go with if you want."

"Sure," Wally said and followed her into the kitchen. "Don't go to any trouble, though."

She rolled her eyes at him and pointed to a pantry cabinet as she pulled a chilled bottle of Chablis from the refrigerator, "I also have some merlot hidden in the cabinet. Would you mind opening one and pouring?"

Carole plated a dish for him and placed it in the microwave to warm and Wally selected the wine glasses. Knowing she like the less fruity and drier Chablis, he poured them each a glass and with a smile, took the glass to her in the kitchen. He set it on the counter and slipped his arms gently around her waist.

She feigned surprise, but slowly twisted in his arms. He kissed her and held her for a very long moment. He liked the way she felt against him and how she returned the firmness of his embrace.

She laid her head against his shoulder and he could feel her slow breathing. "I'm so glad you said 'hello' that day in Hap's."

"I am too," he said and kissed the top of her head. Then he relaxed his hold and asked, "What else can I do?"

Reluctantly, she straightened up. "You can get the salad makings and dressing out. This will be ready in just a few minutes."

"Okay," he smiled and turned to the refrigerator.

▲

"This is really good," Wally said when he started eating. "Sorry to be eating your leftovers, though."

"Thanks. I don't mind," she said as she settled in the chair across from him and then asked, "What had you so busy today that you couldn't take time to eat?"

"The Official story is that while I was meeting with Thom, Ted and Dan this morning, I got an urgent call to come up to the mill." He took a sip of his wine. "The head of Shipping and Receiving got himself electrocuted."

Carole's face went ashen. "Dead?"

He nodded as he slowly spun the wine glass stem between his fingers.

"How'd he get electrocuted?" she asked softly.

Wally waited a long moment, staring at the glass before he leaned forward and reached for her hand. Confused, she took his and watched his expression.

"He wasn't, was he?" she asked, almost in a whisper.

Wally shook his head, but smiled at her. "The 'real' story is a little different. After we'd secured the body with the EMS team from the hospital, Thom went to take care of the 'official' paperwork at the coroner's office. Gary took me aside and told me that Shar and Jill had come to the mill so Jill could talk to her dad."

Carole held his eyes and waited.

"Lou apparently saw Jill when she went into the main office building," he continued, "and Gary thinks he acted out of some kind of loyalty to the missing Judge Bernice."

"What... did he do?" Carole asked softly.

"Gary said Lou casually walked through the offices and down the hall to Jack's office. He shot Jill and Jack from the hallway before Shar could stop him."

Carole stood bolt upright, her chair tumbling noisily behind her.

"They're okay," Wally said as he rose with her, still holding her hand. "They're okay. Shar got him."

"They're both okay?"

"Yes," Wally confirmed. "Shar called Greg and between them and Major Kooich and Leeana and I don't know how many others, they cleaned up the office and took both Jill and Jack back to the ranch."

"To the ranch?" Carole looked very confused. "Not the hospital?"

"No. The hospital would ask too many questions. I went out to the ranch after I finished talking with Gary," Wally continued, shaking his head. "Greg let me visit with them both. Apparently, there's some kind of advanced medical treatment and recuperation system on their ships. Jack was wounded in one arm and he was in one Medical unit, as they called it, and Jill was in another."

"Jack was wounded in one arm?"

"Yeah," he said, "Jill took the brunt of both shots. Something about the suit she wore protected her. Greg said it's a lot like my jackets. Jack doesn't have one of them."

"But she's okay?"

"Yes," he slowly smiled. "She was knocked out and has a few face and neck burns, but Shar insists they won't be noticeable when she comes out of Medical. Jack should be up and around soon."

Carole pondered the news. "You're sure?" Then she took a deep breath and continued when he nodded, "With all of that going on today, I'll bet you've also been searching for clues to help you predict who poses the greatest threats in your spare time." She eyed him suspiciously.

"You know me," he said with a shrug.

"Yes," she said and came around the table and hugged him tightly. "Yes, I do. Thanks for checking up on them and for telling me."

"Of course," he said as he slowly released her and turned to pick up the plate and utensils.

He cleared the table, righted her chair and then settled on the couch while Carole went to change.

"You know," he said when Carole returned, set her wine glass on the end table and curled up beside him. "I just noticed today that they've put up Christmas decorations all over town."

"Happens this time of year," Carole said, surprised.

"I suppose. I was surprised I hadn't noticed sooner," he said as he wrapped his arm around her.

"So," Carole said as she snuggled closer. "Aside from your busy day, have you found out any background on your new deputies?"

"As a matter of fact," Wally said, "I have uncovered a lot about my deputies." He slowly explained what Greg had told him when they met at Rose's place on Tuesday, that the three deputies were handpicked by the Peace Force and 'tagged' like him. "You felt unsure of Dan, right?"

"Yeah. I felt like something was wrong with him or he was uncertain about something," she answered as she slipped her arm around behind him.

"Uncertain might be a good word," Wally agreed and she looked up at him. "It turns out that Dan's married and has a young daughter, early school age. His last assignment kept them apart for nearly a year and he had just gotten back to see them when he was urgently assigned here, indefinitely."

"Oh, Wally. That's terrible," Carole said and sat up. "How long's he going to be here?"

"Indefinitely," Wally repeated.

Carole waited, knowing he had more to say.

"I had Bill start looking for houses for them," Wally continued, "and he found three temporary apartments. He said he should have permanent houses by the end of the week and today he told Thom and Ted he had arranged places for them.

They can move Saturday."

"And Dan?"

"Well, as soon as I found out he was married," Wally smiled, "I asked Bill to look for at least a two bedroom for him. That meant the one Bill had already found wouldn't do, so he's checking on another, more suitable place. He might know by tomorrow or Saturday."

"At least a two bedroom?" Carole smiled. "Are you thinking what I'm thinking?"

Wally smiled. "I told Dan this afternoon, when I got back from Shar's ranch, that he should tell his wife to pack up and to join him here."

Carole snuggled and squeezed him tightly. "Yes, yes. That's great. Is he going to?"

"I don't think there's any question. He'll feel much better once they're here," Wally said.

"And don't give him the late shifts," Carole said firmly, poking him in the ribs, "At least not for a few months."

▲ ▲ ▲ ▲ ▲

Greg met Kiile, Major Kooich and Leeana in the Ready Room at Obscure about an hour after Shara and Jill left with STSX to take Jim Woods back to Lynchburg. Kiile offered him a mug of coffee as he entered and realized Major Kooich and Leeana were already there.

"Good morning, Colonel," Kiile said as he gestured to a chair near Major Kooich. "We have some good news that I thought you'd like to hear."

"So you said," Greg remarked and tasted the coffee. "Then I have something to discuss as well."

"Certainly," Kiile agreed. "Do you want to go first?"

"No. You called us," Greg said.

Kiile tapped his notepad and scrolled to the appropriate

spot. "We have completed a pretty thorough investigation of the fighter we captured," Kiile started, "Thanks to both of you and your fighter group. And we were able to interrogate the cloaking and shield systems onboard." He paused and sipped his coffee. "We have deciphered the maintenance codes and tested them. The code can be sent empathically and the cloaking transmitter responds."

Kiile looked at the broad smiles from all three of them.

"So we now have a Kyddellan code to go with our other codes?" Greg asked. "Is that what you are saying?"

"Yes, Colonel," he replied.

"That's great," Leeana said. "Now we just need one more."

"What?" Greg, Kiile and Major Kooich turned and looked at her. "One more?"

"Yes," she said smugly. "KKLC14, STSX and myself have been analyzing the differences between our Marks and have found there is a progression that follows the Mark numbers. Only a couple of pieces in the codes change from one Mark to the next."

Greg slowly smiled, understanding Leeana. "Is it consistent?" he asked.

"Yes," she confirmed. "If we know the cloaking unit designation, like out Mark numbers, and we have more than one, it is likely that we can find a similar difference and then, possibly, predict the code for units in between, before or after the units interrogated." She looked at Kiile. "Did you get a version or progression ID for the unit on the captured ship?"

"A Version Fifty-Two," Kiile said with a smile. "We also confirmed a diagnostic command the unit accepts, so we can use Shara's trick to drop their veils."

"Did you discover anything more from the fighter?" Major Kooich asked.

"Some," Kiile admitted, "but most of the equipment is similar to ours, different manufacture and some differences in controls layout. Armament is two forward firing cannons, one dual cannon belly turret. Two pulse lasers for lighter targets. We have a listing of their communications channels and acceptance codes from their standard equipment as well as their IFF equipment."

"Do you have anyone that can recode the IFF?" Greg asked.

Kiile looked at him in surprise. "I suppose so. What are you thinking?"

"I am wondering if we can transmit a suitable IFF signature with our equipment," Greg explained, "but most of all, whether the code can be altered so the ship configuration or Class ID is not broadcast."

"Are you thinking," Major Kooich asked, picking up on Greg's idea, "we could use their codes to our benefit in an attack?"

"Possibly," Greg said with a smile. "We can already get in close, but there could be a need to gain entry somewhere and the IFF identification could be helpful."

"I'll get someone on it right away, Colonel," Kiile said. "Oh, and I've sent the packet with the new codes to KKLC14 and to STSX1."

"Anything more?" Greg asked.

"Yes," Kiile grinned. "The pilot was dispatched out of a port under Prince Kiese's control and dropped by a Traders' transport in near space. He gave us a number of names in the Traders Union that were associated with his mission. But the most important detail was that his mission was at the direct request of Chairman Sorgat, the head man at the Union."

"Very good," Greg replied.

"The second name you need to know is Director Korveel, Merchandise," Kiile added. "He is most likely the head man in the handling and distribution of the incoming slaves. I'll send you a complete file of our interrogation."

"Thanks Kiile," Greg said, smiling at Major Kooich and Leeana. "I will get this information to the director as soon as I've looked it over. Do you have anything more?" When Kiile shook his head, Greg continued, "Okay. To my topic. On one occasion STSX was able to collect and carry another ship."

Major Kooich and Leeana nodded, remembering their rescue when STSX carried them back to the Rings for repair.

"Kiile, what I want to know," Greg said very softly, seriously, "is whether you can rig up a means for the Q-Ships to carry the patrol fighters on long sorties, and to be able to deploy and recover them at the battle scene, without inflicting any damage to them in the process."

Kiile's eyes went wide and Major Kooich started to chuckle.

Greg continued, "I would actually prefer to have them under slung to keep the top turrets clear while conveying them."

"I'm certain we can come up with something," Kiile said slowly.

"How soon?" Greg asked before Kiile could ask him the same question.

"I'll... I'll let you know after I talk with my Techs, Colonel," Kiile said, pushing the surprise out of his voice. "I may have an estimate by tomorrow or the next day. I'll let you know."

Saturday, December 17

"Major?" Greg asked as he refilled his cup from the carafe on the table. Matti and Cara had cleared the breakfast dishes, leaving the sweet breads and an extra carafe for their discussion. "How are the nav-com's taking to the new training requirements?" He saw Leeana's expression light up.

"Better than I would have imagined," Major Kooich said. "Each and every one of them seems to have a knack, almost a penchant quality."

"Good. Very good," Greg said softly. "I was hoping that might be the case."

"Hoping?" Major Kooich asked, surprised.

"Yes." He looked at Leeana and continued. "Each nav-com

has many hours in their ships and I suspect that many of them watch what their majors do when they are not tied to a monitor or managing various duties in the back. Like Shara said, both jobs are necessary, but the flying is definitely more exciting."

Major Kooich smiled and thought a moment. "I guess you may be right," he said and glanced at Leeana's smile. "You certainly seem to enjoy the training."

"Very much," she admitted.

"I wish," Major Kooich continued, "that I had thought about that earlier. All of those years with you stuck in the back."

"I wasn't stuck," Leeana said firmly. "It's my primary job, thank you very much."

Greg laughed and sipped his coffee.

"Shara and I are going up for a while this morning," Greg said. "Are any of the cadets free for a couple of hours? I'd like to start getting them used to flying escort."

"I think Tigs and Moss are free," the Major said. "When and where do you want them to rendezvous?"

⁂

Casi slowed STSX to a hover south of Obscure at an altitude just above the Spires in the Western Rim Mountains. She saw STSX's display of the patrol fighters as they ascended from under Obscure's veil and shield dome.

"Show them where we are, STSX," she said as they climbed.

"THEY KNOW."

"Thanks. Open scrambled communications, please," she said and continued. "Apache Patrol Three and Four. Join me on both flanks and stay close."

"Will do, Apache Leader," the very young feminine voice of eighteen year old Cadet Tigs in Apache Three replied as Casi pushed the power levers up and accelerated into to a climb.

"Roger," Cadet Moss agreed from Apache Patrol Four as they closed formation and broke out of the solid overcast that covered most of the northern United States and all of Canada.

Casi turned and looked over her shoulder at Stran in the nav-com console chair. "I'll pace the space station for a little while and let them get the feel of orbital operations."

"That's good, Bren," he said and glanced at her, quickly going back to his monitor. "Give them a good look at the planet while they're up. I'll come forward after I discuss some thoughts with the director."

"Thanks," she said and turned her thoughts back to the cadets. "Apache Patrol Three and Four, we will rendezvous with the manned space station as it passes over the west coast of South America. We will approach from the north, with the station on our right. Q-TTYF8 and Q-LTVC21 are its present escorts."

Then she remembered another aspect of her training. "Apache Patrol Three and Four. Weapons Check. Your ship has two forward firing fixed cannons and one dual cannon turret. Pick a clear sector of space and fire one short range burst from each canon, individually. Apache Patrol Three fire now."

If there was any surprise in the patrol fighter cockpits, it was not apparent as Patrol Three pulsed four bolts into the void to STSX's left.

"Apache Patrol Four fire now."

Patrol Four complied and Casi watched the bursts disappear into the distance to their right.

They flew in silence as they climbed south, closing on the space station's course as it fell around the planet. When she felt the station come over the horizon behind them and to their right, Casi told STSX to match speed and position the flight with the station twenty miles a beam on their right.

"TTYF8," she said on the communications link. "STSX1 approaching from your left. Flight of three." Then to STSX she said, "Show them where we are, but do not drop our veil or Sensor blocking."

"DONE."

"Thanks, STSX."

"We have you," Major Mooren's voice replied. "All's quiet here. What brings you up on such a wonderful day?"

"We needed some sunshine," she said. "We have two cadets up for familiarization."

TTYF8 hesitated a long moment before he replied. "Best IP's a cadet could ask for," he finally said.

Casi caught his underlying question, wondering why the campaign commander would spend time with the cadets instead of leaving it to the cadet instructors. "The colonel wanted some private time with the director and since we were coming up, we figured it was a good opportunity for the cadets."

"Yes, Ma'am," Major Mooren said, "it certainly is."

Casi turned and looked at Stran again. "We're stable twenty miles out, love. I'm going to bring us in closer."

"Almost done Bren," he said. She could feel his focus on the communications but did not try to listen to his thoughts.

"Do you have TTYF8 and LTVC21's positions?" she asked STSX.

"YES. THEY ARE ONE MILE ON EACH SIDE OF S.S. QUICKSILVER."

"Okay. Let's close in until they are two miles on our right."

⬥

Casi had settled her flight of three in the anticipated position and began answering questions from the cadets as they arose. Greg finished with the director and came forward during Casi's explanation of why the Force has taken on the role of protecting the station. He grinned and remembered how excited Casi had been the first time he brought her up into space and she saw the station. To see it for the first time, close up had been a highlight he did not think she would ever forget.

After nearly a half an hour on station, Casi opened the com link. "TTYF8. STSX is taking the flight of three and breaking formation."

⬥

"Safe trip STSX1," Major Mooren said and watched their computer generated target slowly separate from the normal cluster of three. "They're away Franni."

"I feel like I should have said 'hello' or something," she admitted. "But I couldn't think of anything appropriate."

"Just 'hello' would have been fine," he said. "I think Lieutenant Casi would have liked that."

"Maybe, but I'm sure glad you didn't say anything about her 'babysitting' the cadets." she said with a chuckle.

Major Mooren slowly turned the pilot's chair around to aft facing and stared at the back of her nav-com console chair. *'You heard that?'* he asked softly in his mind.

"Yes. And you..." She stopped when she realized he had not spoken out loud.

Slowly she turned her chair to face him, a sheepish smile on her face.

"How long have you been *hearing* me, Franni?" he asked softly out loud.

She looked down a moment and then back at him. "About nine or ten days, I think."

Slowly a grin crossed his face and grew into a smile. "I'm honored Franni," he said sincerely. "Very honored."

"Can you *hear* me?" she asked, uncertain if she should.

"Yes, when you let me," he said. "That is, when you don't close your mind to others."

"I... I guess I do keep my own council a lot," she admitted and looked at the floor again.

"As it should be," he agreed. "But Franni, I want you to know that you may *speak* to me any time you wish."

She looked up and smiled. "Thank you." Then she asked, "How long?"

"About three weeks," he admitted. Then as he turned his chair back to forward facing, he said, *'I like hearing you.'*

She knew her cheeks were getting red. *'Thanks'* she said and quickly turned back to her console.

⋏ ⋏ ⋏ ⋏ ⋏

"Colonel Townsley," Ensign Riviera, S.S. QuickSilver's Surveillance Specialist said into her boom microphone.

"This is Townsley. What have you got Ensign?" the watch commander asked.

"The Scanners just picked up eight upper spectral energy spikes below us and to our northeast," she said softly.

"I'm on my way," he said. "What sort of spikes?"

"I'll show you when you get here," she answered and closed the connection.

⋏

Colonel Thomas Townsley was the person between Admiral Baker and the rest of the multinational space station, S.S. QuickSilver. He was responsible for knowing about all things happening in the daily routines on board and for coordinating any and all responses for those things abnormal that happened concerning the station. In the past few months, with the attempted intervention of all communications and systems control by an off-world slave trading organization, the appearance of the ominous other-worldly battlecruiser intent on commandeering the station, and the arrival of the nearly invisible corsairs that destroyed it, Colonel Townsley's sphere of responsibility had been greatly expanded beyond the composite and titanium structure of the station.

Within minutes of Ensign Riviera's call, Colonel Townsley drifted down the central core and into the adjacent surveillance and tracking chamber. Ensign Riviera's observation station, relocated from the main Bridge, allowed her to monitor the unusual events that continued to arise around them without attracting the attention of the rest of the Bridge crew.

"What have you got, Ensign," Colonel Townsley asked as he grabbed the hand rail that encircled the vertically facing display screen. He stopped opposite the Ensign as she looked up and keyed a sequence on the keypad to her right.

"About ten minutes ago," she began and gestured to a section of the down-looking, full color display, "in this area there were two sets of four energy streaks each with a length of about five miles. The spectrum matches with the spectrum we recorded when the corsairs attacked the battlecruiser back on the twentieth of October."

"The corsairs?" he asked in surprise. "Are there more attacking something else?"

"I don't think so," she said as the slow motion replay ran in the display. "Two groups of streaks, like from two corsairs, assuming they were corsairs."

"Well Admiral Baker did say we were going to have unseen escorts," he said, smiling to ease his heightened concerns.

"Yes, sir," she said and paused the image. "My fiancé is an old war video buff, sir. And the other night we were watching another old one with lots of fighter planes. If he saw these images, I think he'd say they look like the ships were clearing their weapons."

"Clearing their weapons?"

"You know, sir. Checking them out to be sure everything worked before going into combat," she said, studying his expression. "They weren't firing at anything specific and all the traces were parallel, short range."

"You and your Wilson might have something there, Ensign," Colonel Townsley said with a sincere smile. "Maybe it's something tangible for us to show that we do still have escorts around us."

"Yes sir," she smiled weakly in return. "There's also a smattering of something at the high edges of our communications frequencies."

Colonel Townsley's expression stiffened.

"Telnet caught a faint glimpse of an unintelligible conversation, probably scrambled," she said and keyed for a replay. "The first is just before the first set of streaks, then again in between the two sets, and then afterwards."

He listened to the faint, wavering sounds, but obviously could not discern any more than the experts had already. Then Colonel Townsley pushed himself into a more upright position, thanked the ensign and turned to the central core tube and the multiple tubes that connected with the outer rings.

▲

Colonel Townsley walked slowly into Admiral Baker's anteroom in the middle ring, where the spin of the station afforded a partial gravity and with a little practice, most people were able to maintain some semblance of proper poise and dignity in moving from place to place.

"Good morning Anne," he greeted Lieutenant Anne Wardly, Admiral Baker's secretary and personal assistant since before he earned the position of Chief Officer on earth's first, fully manned, permanent space station.

"Good Morning, Tom," she replied as he stopped before her desk.

"Is the admiral in?" he asked and she got up to announce him. She returned quickly and gestured for him to go in.

"He was about to call for you," she said with a smile as he passed. "Your timing is very good."

"Admiral," he said as he stopped inside the large office and waited.

"Come in," Admiral Baker said and gestured to a chair in front of his desk. "Good of you to come. I just asked Anne to call for you."

"So Anne said, sir," he said as he took the proffered chair. "What can I do for you?"

"I've received another very odd communiqué from QuickSilver Communications," the admiral said and off handedly gestured to the floor, meaning the planet below. "It seems QCC has sent a request from Captain Jim Woods."

"Captain? I thought your last communiqués were from a

Lieutenant Woods," Colonel Townsley said, thinking out loud.

"Yes. One and the same," Admiral Baker added, "so I am told. He is requesting a meeting—"

"A meeting?" Colonel Townsley interrupted in surprise. "Sorry sir."

"Yes, a meeting," Admiral Baker continued, "a meeting between myself and the campaign commander leading the fight against the off world forces. He is a Colonel Geaardt of an organization called the Galactic Peace Force. Both of us are to bring our key staff members to the meeting."

Colonel Townsley sagged back into his chair. "How does he propose you hold a meeting? And where?"

"Here," the admiral said, pointing to the floor.

Colonel Townsley was again surprised, but he held his composure. "And the topic of this meeting is?"

"To propose and implement improvements in the station's defenses and target tracking and recognition."

Colonel Townsley stared at the admiral, certain his mouth had fallen open, but was happy to discover it was not actually agape when he tried to close it.

"The request says," Admiral Baker continued, "they would also like an audience with the surveillance officer that has been secretly observing and tracking their activities over the past couple of months, the maintenance officer that is responsible for the station's maneuvering systems and the weapons control officer that will have authority over the defenses of the station."

"Wow," Colonel Townsley said softly. "They know a lot more about us than we know about them."

"Yes, but this is too intriguing of an offer to refuse," Admiral Baker said as he scrolled the information on his computer monitor.

"When, if I may ask?" Colonel Townsley asked.

"Monday, 1400 Eastern Standard Time," Admiral Baker said softly. "How would you propose we keep their arrival secret, Tom?"

"That could be difficult," Colonel Townsley said, "but if we secure the shuttle docking bays in the upper core, move the personnel out except for a couple to handle the airlocks and booms... sir? Can they couple with our docking rings?"

"No. They cannot," Admiral Baker admitted. "The request says they prefer to transfer EVA through our personnel airlocks."

"Okay, that might actually be for the best. We can still bring them in through the shuttle docking facilities. They can park above the rings where their ships can only be seen from the docks." Colonel Townsley smiled. He felt good about the solution, then a thought struck him. "Sir, what if this is another attempt to take over the station?"

"I thought about that, Tom," the admiral said. "It could be, but if this was a hostile attempt, I hardly think they would go through QCC and Captain Woods. I also don't think we could stop them if we wanted to."

"Just the same," Colonel Townsley said, "I'd like the authority to have a few armed security Marines on standby. For the protection of our 'guests.'"

"Only if they know I will not let us be the aggressors," Admiral Baker said firmly. "I believe these are the people that have saved our bacon and kept us out of the fire."

"Yes, sir. Understood, sir," Colonel Townsley said and nodded. He took a deep breath. "I will be sure there is no misunderstanding that we are receiving very important allies and only need support if something goes wrong."

"Thank you Tom," the admiral said, still holding Tom's eyes. "I believe everything is riding on our trusting these people. We can't afford to blow this one."

Colonel Townsley nodded and thought a few moments before he spoke again. "Sir? A thought comes to me that it will not look very proper if we present our key surveillance expert and interpreter of shadows and wavers as a mere 'Ensign.'"

Admiral Baker looked at Townsley, startled. Slowly his expression turned to a smile. "I think you are most certainly right, Colonel." He keyed the console on his desk. "Anne, if you have a moment."

Lieutenant Anne Wardly stepped in quickly. "Sir?"

"Anne, I need you to have Ensign Riviera, Surveillance, report to me quietly and on the double," he said with a huge smile.

"Yes sir," she said and slipped back through the door.

When she was gone, the admiral looked at Colonel Townsley and asked, "Lieutenant Junior Grade?"

Colonel Townsley slowly shook his head. "Lieutenant. With all of the trimmings, honors and privileges."

Admiral Baker nodded. "All right Tom. Now, what was it that brought you up here before I could call for you?"

"Ensign Riviera," he said with a huge smile and proceeded to explain what she had seen and heard.

Eighty-Two

Sunday, December 18

A little morning sunshine was peeking through holes in the clouds, but the tall pines kept the streets, yards and houses covered in shadows as Wally stopped in front of Carole's house. The streets were still snow packed and icy. At the front door, he knocked and waited for her to answer. When she didn't, he knocked again a little harder and after another long moment, the garage door began to open.

"Morning Wally," Carole said as the door stopped at the top of its swing. With a sack in each arm, wearing jeans, a long sleeved flannel shirt and the green sleeveless, fitted vest he liked very much, she turned toward the door into the house. "I thought I heard someone knocking. Come on in. I had to run up to the Stop 'N Shop for a couple of things 'someone' made me forget when I got off work last night. Just got back."

He followed and opened the door for her as the garage door closed behind them.

"Now, I didn't have anything to do with your forgetfulness," he said, pleading innocence.

"Like heck you didn't," she smiled as she set the bags on the counter. Then she turned, reached up and threw her arms around his neck. "You know very well everything else went completely out of my head when I saw you last night," she said and kissed him fully, pulling him as close as she could while standing on her toes. Slowly he tightened his embrace, straightened up and held her against him for a long moment.

As he set her back on her feet, he asked what he could do to help with breakfast. After a brief discussion of options, Wally threw together a baked egg dish with various vegetables, cheeses, meats and seasonings while Carole made fresh biscuits and white, spiced gravy.

Settled at the table, Carole started eating and smiled at her first bite. "I can't get over what you can do with eggs."

"Thanks," he said and poured her a cup of coffee.

They were nearly finished eating when she asked, "What's on your agenda today?"

"Unfortunately," he said with a sip of his coffee, "I have to head over to the capital about noon."

"The capital?" she asked with a raised eyebrow, "Something up?"

"No. I just have to pick up some new equipment, uniforms and such stuff," he said. "Leaving around noon will get me in there early evening, but this way I can have the morning with you."

"Are you going to be there all day tomorrow?" she asked.

She stacked her plates and set them aside, he placed his plates on top of hers.

"The official things I have to do will go into the afternoon," he said. "Depending on how it goes, I might be able to start back before it gets too late. If not, I'll start back Tuesday morning at the latest."

"Is the trip because of your promotion?"

"Yup," he said as he picked up the plates and utensils and took them to the kitchen. He placed them in the sink to let them soak, then returned to the table to finish his coffee, "A lot of paperwork, a little research, and meetings with a number of people in the Law Enforcement Commission."

"Sounds like a lot of fun," she chuckled. "Glad it's you and not me."

"Oh, I meant to tell you," he said as he finished the pot of coffee. "Dan got a nice three bedroom place, a couple of blocks from the Elementary School. It has a fenced backyard with a lot of space for his daughter to play in."

"Nice," she said, smiling. "Has he started moving in?"

"Today," Wally said. "I think he said his wife and daughter will be here for Christmas."

"Wonderful."

They chatted about Carole's plans for the day, washed and dried the dishes and then drove out to her father's ranch to tend to her horse Jesse. At Rusty's persistent invitation, he delayed his departure to have lunch with Carole and her folks. Afterwards, he insisted he had to go and Carole walked him out to his jeep.

"Mom was serious about having you and the deputies come out for Christmas dinner. My sister called and said she and Carrie Anne will be here for the week," Carole said as they stopped beside his jeep and he collected his utility belt and pistol from the locked box in the back.

Once he had fastened them around his waist, he smiled. "I'll be here. I think I can arrange our schedules to let everyone have some time off. And I certainly want to spend the time with you."

"Stay out of those fancy beer halls," she said softly with a smile. "And be safe."

"I'll do my best," he said. He gently pulled her close and kissed her. "See you as soon as I get back."

She watched the drive long after his jeep had turned onto the county road and disappeared behind the trees to the east. She knew he would be all right, but she still worried.

▲ ▲ ▲ ▲ ▲

By late afternoon, the broken overcast had given way and only a few scattered clouds remained over Riggs Valley and by full dark, the brilliant starry night sky dominated the heavens. Deputy Ted Marks casually drove around the town, crossing Main along River and past the hospital, then down to the college and back along Cedar to Cleary. He zigzagged back east on Juniper and then down behind the elementary and high school campus on Hurst to Walnut.

His evening rounds took him back across Main and into the residential area to the west on Spruce and up Donovan. He turned west to quiet Newly at the west edge of town, then up and back east to the marshal's office on Ash. As expected on a Sunday night, everything was peaceful and he planned one pass by the office and then down Main to check out the businesses and the crowd at Hap's Place before he found a visible spot to park and wait for his next scheduled rounds.

As he slowly drove past the north side of the office, he caught the movement of a silhouette slip around the south end of the building. Puzzled, he tapped his earpiece and asked the remote to visually record anything it saw in that area and he turned into the front parking lot. Rounding the building to the back without seeing anyone, he figured that whoever it was had gone on south, either to the next business or on toward the city hall grounds.

"Dan," he said into the short boom mic. "I'm going out on foot. Someone may have been snooping around the office. I'm going to check it out."

"I'm coming south from mill," Dan's voice answered as he closed and locked the cruiser's door. "I'll be there in a minute."

Ted climbed the steps slowly, checking the shadows, shining his hand lamp behind the shrubbery along the building. He twisted the door handle and sighed; it was still locked. He was checking the windows across the back of the building when Dan pulled in and stopped behind his cruiser.

"Find anything?" Dan asked as he got out and stood beside his patrol car.

"Yeah," Ted said and held out his hand.

Dan locked his car door and walked over to see what Ted was holding. He instantly recognized the small, recording transmitter.

"Is it live?" Dan asked in a whisper.

"No," Ted smiled, "Not anymore." He showed Dan the transmitter's open back and the loose battery. "I think we need to check all of the other windows and anywhere one of these

114

might be hiding."

"Better keep a check on our patrol cars," Dan added as he glanced at them.

"Good thought," Ted agreed and then tapped his earpiece. "WL-One, can you scan for transmitters, wire taps, tracking devices?"

"YES," the answer came to both of them.

"Very nice," Dan said softly.

"WL-One," Ted said, taking the initiative. "Please scan the perimeter of the office and all three of our patrol cars."

After a few minutes in which Ted figured the remote was traveling to execute his request, the remote reported, "OFFICE IS CLEAN. DEPUTY LUPIS' PATROL CAR IS CLEAN. DEPUTY MARKS' PATROL CAR IS CLEAN. DEPUTY BAINES' PATROL CAR HAS A SINGLE TRANSMITTER AND ONE TRACKING BEACON UNDER THE DRIVER'S FLOOR BOARD."

"WL-One," Ted continued when he controlled his surprise. "Please scan the Office and the patrol cars every time we start a shift, mid-shift and again at the end of the shifts. Report if you find anything."

"WILL COMPLY."

"WL-One?" Ted asked again. "Were you able to follow the person I saw?"

"YES. THE PERSON WENT EAST ON BIRCH, SOUTH ON ESTER AND ONTO THE COLLEGE CAMPUS. THE PERSON WAS NEAR THE STUDENT UNION WHEN DEPUTY MARKS REQUESTED WL-ONE SCAN THE OFFICE AND PATROL CARS."

Ted shrugged as he looked at Dan's wide smile. "I guess I should have checked on what it was doing first."

"Even with that, I think I like having a remote around," Dan said as he headed back to his cruiser. "Off to Thom's?"

"Yes," Ted agreed. "He comes on at two in the morning this week, so we'll have to tell him what's up when we see him in the morning."

⋏

They stopped on Kelly next door to Thom's new place just above Quincy and Dan kept watch while Ted looked under the driver's side of Thom's patrol car. With a quick flash of his hand light, he spotted the voice transmitter and quickly disabled it. Then he looked up at Dan. "Got the transmitter, and... now the tracker," he said as he pried the unit from the floorboard.

"What do you think we should do with the tracker?" Dan asked. "Besides throwing it into the river."

"Nah, don't want to do that," Ted said with a smile. "It's evidence. I'm going to collect them and store them in the office safe. That's assuming we will find more. When Wally gets back, he can decide if we have any uses for them.

⋏ ⋏ ⋏ ⋏ ⋏

Matti and Cara finished clearing the dining room table after a light Sunday evening meal as Major Kooich and Leeana found their way to the loveseat left of the fireplace. Leeana curled her legs under her and snuggled with the major's arm wrapped around her shoulders. Nick and Jill had taken places on the long couch, Greg was in his favorite overstuffed chair opposite the loveseat and Cheral was in the overstuffed chair at the end of the long couch when Shara came out of the kitchen.

"I'd like you and KKLC14 as part of our escort," Greg was saying when Shara sat on his lap facing the group and draped her legs over the arm of the chair.

"You're not expecting trouble, are you?" Leeana asked.

"Not exactly," Greg answered. "But I'm not going to ignore the possibility. Our arrival will be a shock to almost everyone that sees us and I just want to be ready if someone reacts the wrong way." Then he looked back at Major Kooich. "Who will you have with you?"

"Well, Colonel," Major Kooich started slowly, thinking of

his options. "I would take TTYF8 and KVWC33 and the cadets. Patrol Fighter Four is having some issues and the mechanics have been working on it since early this morning. If they can't get it fixed, I'll just have cadets Two and Three," he glanced at Cheral's smile, "to provide a visual presence. That will keep LTVC21 and MKCC5 available as back up if anything happens that we can't handle. All of the ships are banded, which will give us a unified squadron appearance."

"Very good," Greg said.

He was about to continue when Matti and Cara stopped in the dining room with a tray and coffee. He nodded and Cara set the tray stand near the loveseat and Matti began pouring for each of them.

When they had finished, Greg continued, "If anything does happen that you can't handle, and if we can't get back to STSX1, you take yourself, Leeana and KKLC14 and withdraw. The baton will pass to you to continue the Campaign."

Major Kooich nodded, ignored the serious implications of Greg's acknowledgement and continued, "Who are you going to take onboard with you?"

"Shara and I will take Kiile and we will pick up Jim in Lynchburg on our way," Greg said and took a sip of his coffee. "Jim says the response was pleasant and seemed appropriate for the circumstances."

"I think four is a good number, Colonel," Major Kooich agreed. "It won't seem too intimidating."

Greg was about to comment when he felt Shara stiffen.

'There's a new sensation, love. Lots of people and... and I think one large ship and four or five smaller ones.'

He looked at her, puzzled. *'I don't feel them yet.'*

'They're very high, across the planet. They seem to be parked, but I can't be sure. They feel too far away.'

"What is it?" Leeana asked, seeing the change in Greg and Shara's mood.

"Shara feels some new presences," Greg explained.

"Greg," Shara said out loud. "I'm going to take Cheral with me and go see what's there." She was already on her feet before he could respond, but she could feel his concern and turned to face him. "No engagements. Just taking a look. You keep on with the mission planning and I'll let you know what we see."

Greg caught her hand and stood up before she could turn and leave. He pulled her to him in a quick, gentle hug and then let her go. *'Be safe, Bren. No one-man stands.'*

She smiled, remembering the last time she went solo, chasing Ahaar and discovering the small fleet of battlecruisers and fighters. *'No one-man stands, love. If it's trouble, I'll call for backup.'*

Shara nodded to Cheral and started through the dining room, but stopped and turned. "Come on, Jill. Get your Blues." Then to Cheral she continued, "If you need them, we still have one set of your Blues onboard," she said as they grabbed their coats.

⚓

Casi and Jill were already changed and Casi was hurrying up the ladder in the central connection chamber before Cheral was half dressed. The significant changes in STSX's configuration had caught Cheral completely by surprise.

Cheral dropped into the aft, double wide cushioned chair and was putting her boots on when she felt STSX move. She realized how much better the chairs and the fold-out table were and wondered why they hadn't thought about that when she was Stran's nav-com. As she started up the ladder to the upper deck, the larger galley caught her eye, another significant improvement in STSX.

At the top, she started to turn to the nav-com chair, but Casi said, "Up here. Use the right jumpseat. STSX will give us the displays up here."

Cheral slid into the new, cushioned jumpseat and smiled as she strapped herself in. Jill was in a jumpseat on the left. "So much has changed since I left," she admitted as Casi lifted them through the ranch's shield barrier and into the evening darkness.

"Yeah," Shara said with a smile. "Greg made a lot of changes after he dropped you off at the academy. That jumpseat is new from when we went for the director's awards dinner. He had the old one put on the left so we can have three seats up front."

"Definitely better."

"STSX," Casi said, "Do you have anything on the targets?"

"NO. THEY ARE SENSOR BLOCKED."

"Put the 3-D Global display up front," Casi said. "Plot the ranch, the space station and the presences I feel."

The 3-D display coalesced to her right, between them and the front cockpit wall, and the requested points appeared.

Casi stared at the distance between the globe and the presences, plotted nearly to the canopy above them. "Is that correct, STSX?" she asked. "They're so far out."

"THE LOCATION OF YOUR PRESENCE IS TWO-HUNDRED AND TEN THOUSAND MILES ABOVE THE PLANET."

"How far?" Jill asked softly to no one in particular.

Casi took a deep breath and looked at Jill and then at Cheral. "Are you ready to see who's visiting today?"

When they smiled, nodded and Cheral said "yeah," Casi said, "STSX, plot us an intercept. I want to circle the cluster and see what's there. Stay Sensor Blocked and Cloaked. Shields Full."

A faint green line spiraled across the 3-D display, and a heads-up reticule appeared between her and the canopy. STSX slowly turned and pitched to track the line.

"I see you've done this before," Cheral chided Casi. "You make it look easy."

Casi felt her cheeks warm, but just said, "Thanks."

"STSX," Cheral said, assuming at least a minor role in the mission, "Weapons status."

"ALL WEAPONS SYSTEMS ARE PEAKED AND ACTIVE. THREE QUAD CANNON TURRETS GREEN, THREE

PULSE-LASERS GREEN, DISPERSIBLE BINS FULL AND SYSTEMS ACTIVE. SHIELDS ON INDEPENDENT POWER, PEAKED AND OPERATING IN THE GREEN. SHIELDS ON STANDARD POWER QUIESCENT. CLOAKING ON INDEPENDENT POWER, PEAKED AND OPERATING IN THE GREEN."

"What does he mean, 'independent' power?" Cheral asked. "Another modification?"

"Yes," Casi said as she pushed the thrust levers past half. "When Greg upgraded STSX and replaced the canon turrets with quad cannons, he also added a second core power module in the right pylon so Cloaking and Shields can be operated completely separate from the ship's normal core power module. We have the ship's original core power and the new core power module available, together or separately. Weapons power can be shared to get the best balance with the ship's other systems." She glanced at Cheral with a smile. "Also gives us a full power back up if one of them is damaged in an engagement. KKLC14 is similarly modified."

"I feel like I'm in a completely different ship," Cheral admitted.

"I'm sure. Greg also modified the engine's upgrade," Casi added. "STSX now has more than double the thrust he had before. We can make the Rings in forty-six terran hours." Casi saw Cheral's mouth drop open.

"FOUR THOUSAND MILES AND CLOSING RAPIDLY," STSX announced and Casi quickly reduced thrust.

"See?" Casi said seeing their stunned faces, "He's fast!" To STSX she said, "I want to circle them at a ten mile radius." Then she thought, *'Greg, can I interrupt?'*

'You're not an interruption. I've been listening.'

'Good. I want you to see what we see.' Then she said out loud, "STSX, record continuous visuals for archive and post flight debriefing."

"ONE HUNDRED MILES AND STILL CLOSING RAPIDLY."

Casi pulled the thrust back and added a little more braking. "Picky, picky," she said and smiled at Cheral. "Can you feel them, Cheral?"

"I sense something, but I couldn't say it was them," she said and twisted her smile in uncertainty.

"Jill?"

Slowly, Jill shook her head.

"Can either of you feel people?"

"Sometimes," Cheral admitted and Jill nodded weakly. "I think I feel the people more right now than I do the ships," Cheral said.

"We need to figure out how to focus those sensations," Casi said absently.

"MEDICAL CAN SHARPEN THOSE IMAGES, CAPTAIN."

Cheral was startled and again had to close her mouth. "You never told me Medical could do that, STSX."

"Maybe you can try after we're done here," Casi said and turned back to her feelings. "We've got one large transport, I think, and seven escorts."

"CORRECT."

"Can we get closer and miss the escorts?" Cheral asked, focusing her attention on the targets.

"YES."

"Okay," Casi continued. "One complete pass at ten miles and then get closer, work our way in as close in as you can."

They watched quietly, as if any noise would alert the transport or escorts to their presence. On the third pass, STSX had worked in to two miles and tilted the axis of his circle to evade the fighters.

"THE TRANSPORT IS PARKED GEOSYNCHRONOUS WITH THE PLANET."

"STSX," Cheral said, "If the transport is parked above a spot on the planet, can you identify that point?"

121

"YES."

"Please identify it in global coordinates," Cheral continued, "and plot it on the display. Archive the information."

"Second display, please, STSX," Casi said. "Enlarge the map to show the point."

A second display coalesced and the image slowly grew, flattening as the point of reference zoomed in closer. Finally, the image stopped and Casi smiled at the clear expanse of ocean. She focused her senses and said, "They're fully cloaked. STSX, display the details I'm sensing."

And as the display changed to full color and details of a very large construction site sharpened, Casi noted the wide, darker circular depression centered in the image. "I think we have found the new launch facility."

"YES. IT APPEARS TO BE A MAN-MADE ISLAND."

'You see this, love?'

'Yes, I do, Bren. Very nice.'

"STSX," Casi said, turning back to the moment and the group of ships they were circling. "Can you light them up?"

After a short moment, blips for the seven fighters appeared on the display.

"FIGHTERS ONLY. MARK TWENTY-TWO CODES. TRANSPORT IS STILL CLOAKED."

"Okay," Casi said, "we can see the fighters if they descend to the surface. We'll have to assume the fighters are following the transport when they move. STSX, please check on the fighters periodically, multiple times each day." She looked at Cheral and Jill. "I think we're done. Let's go home."

"I'm glad," Cheral started, "that was just reconnaissance."

"Since it was a transport and not a battlecruiser," Casi said smiling, "I would expect it to be a short confrontation if it was one, not that confrontations can't go sour, but we have them seriously out gunned,"

"Yeah," Cheral chuckled. "I remember someone saying

you've reset the bar for all of the cadets concerning tactics and the numbers of kills."

"That one was tough," Casi admitted, reflecting deeply on her single handed engagement of the two battlecruisers and what turned out to be fifty-nine fighters when the counting was done. "I didn't know we were winning until it was over. I was very lucky that time."

Cheral smiled. "I'm glad to see you're still down-to-earth, Casi. I always liked that about you."

Casi took a deep breath and smiled. "Now, how much do you trust STSX? Enough to let Medical see if they can help you?"

"I trust STSX more than I trust most people," Cheral said firmly. "And except for my recuperation after Pitcarthy, STSX and this Medical know me better than anyone. Let's see what they think."

Casi was surprised at the eagerness in Cheral's voice and actions.

"Jill, are you willing to let Medical get to know you?" Casi asked, as she swiveled the pilot's chair to aft facing and unbuckled.

"I guess," Jill said and nodded slowly.

"STSX," Casi said as Cheral led the way down through the floor portal into the central chamber and then to the left side Medical couch, "Give Cheral's Medical enough time to finish whatever diagnostics it needs to do before we overfly the new launch facility and start back to the ranch."

Casi watched as Cheral quickly unfastened her Blues and pulled her arm from the sleeve. She positioned the arm band on her upper arm as she settled back on the couch.

"Looks like you've done this before," Casi said as she slipped a thin pillow under Cheral's head, pushed her down onto the couch and pulled the retention netting over her lower torso and legs. Casi keyed the small console on the bulkhead above Cheral's head and waited for Medical to Initialize.

"DIAGNOSTICS COMMENCING. INITIAL ANALYSIS WILL REQUIRE APPROXIMATELY TWELVE POINT FOUR THREE MINUTES."

"Okay, Jill," Casi said turning to her. "On the other couch just like Cheral."

It took Jill a few minutes longer to get situated and comfortable, but when Casi was satisfied, she keyed the console on the bulkhead above Jill's head.

"Thanks, STSX," Casi said and then left Jill and Cheral and both Medicals. She drifted into the galley to fix herself a container of ration tea while she waited.

Eighty-Three
Monday, December 19

Stran, in his dress Blues, complete with all his ribbons, braids, ropes and stars, had seated Captain Jim Woods, wearing his Air Force Service Dress uniform and Squad Leader Kiile, slightly uncomfortable in his Blue Dress uniform, together in the two double wide chairs in STSX's sleeping compartment. Jim was surprised when Kiile had shown up dressed in a uniform other than his usual camos and flop hat. Marine Twelve sat silently on the near end of the right side Medical couch, dressed in his winter white camos.

"Sorry for the surprise, Kiile," Jim said as they sat down. "I didn't realize you were a Chief Warrant Officer."

"I know," Kiile replied. "I usually don't tell people. Simple Squad Leader does just fine." He smiled and watched Stran climb the ladder to the flight deck. Then he whispered to Jim, "I'm glad the colonel let the dress code slip a little and let us bring a weapon."

"Me too," Jim agreed. "I noticed the colonel and the lieutenant both have Brekshiir 710s on their left wrists and at least one Kaaspr. Admiral Baker is an honest soldier and an honest man, true to his word, but I am also certain he has never been faced with something like this before. He has to be on his guard."

STSX began to rise and Jim absently wondered which of them was flying this time. He heard a chuckle drift down from the deck above and then Stran's voice said, "Casi is."

Kiile looked at Jim's astonished expression and said, "Must have been something you said. I didn't ask." Then after a pause, he added, "I don't think a lot gets past the colonel or the lieutenant."

They passed the time with general discussions concerning the cadets and how quickly the colonel had pressed them into service and Jim expressed his understandings of the quick progress they were having with the nav-com pilot training. Kiile was equally impressed and said so.

Jim suddenly realized the ride was shorter than he expected when STSX asked, "CAPTAIN WOODS. DO YOU HAVE THE ADMIRAL'S PRIVATE COMMUNICATIONS FREQUENCY AND ADDRESS?"

"Yes," he said and repeated the information.

A couple of minutes passed and then STSX said, "WE WILL PARK NEAR THE SHUTTLE AIRLOCKS AT THE SPACE SIDE OF THE MAIN CORE TUBE IN FIVE."

Stran stepped out of the central compartment and drifted to a stop beside Jim. "We need to get into our EVA costumes. Casi will join us as soon as STSX parks and Major Kooich has our squadron in position."

⏶

Admiral Baker and Colonel Townsley waited in the shuttle receiving area, just inside the Shuttle Airlock Number One. The admiral glanced at Colonel Townsley and checked his watch.

"Ten minutes," he said softly, even though they were the only two in the chamber.

Colonel Townsley looked around the chamber, and at the expansive view beyond the almost continuous ring of windows around the outer wall, broken only where the two airlocks and the two service tubes reached out from the station's central core.

Admiral Baker twitched, almost startled when his remote communicator buzzed.

"Admiral," Lieutenant Wardly's voice said. "Our guests have reported they are five minutes from parking. Lieutenant Riviera says she has nothing on the scanners."

"Thank you Anne," the admiral said and disconnected as

126

he looked out through the windows. "They must be close. Is everything secure?"

"Yes, sir," Colonel Townsley said as he slowly turned to check the view.

They waited the long five minutes and the admiral's communicator buzzed again.

"Admiral," Lieutenant Wardly said, "They are parked. They are a flight of six and will drop their cloaking in one minute, but they claim we will still not be able to pick them up on our scanners."

"Thank you, Anne," the admiral said.

Before she disconnected, she added, "They will be bringing five persons through the airlock from the colonel's ship. The other ships will remain in a protective escort ring around us." The communicator disconnected.

"Protection for who?" Colonel Townsley asked. "For us or for them?"

"Tom!" the admiral snapped. "Stow that! These are people that have shown us they are our allies. They did not have to help us, and they certainly did not have to come and discuss their intentions with us." The admiral held Colonel Townsley's eyes firmly. "I agreed to being ready for trouble, but DO NOT presuppose they are THE trouble."

"Yes, sir. Sorry, sir," Colonel Townsley said and looked out of the window again. He stared in disbelief at the sleek, crisp lines of the matte grey fighter parked with its right side facing the station.

"Get a look at that," he said in a whisper as Admiral Baker stared beside him. "There are three more like that one, well, the same but with different canopies, and two smaller fighters with them. They all have the same red marking."

"They don't look anything like the two fighters Ensign, I mean, Lieutenant Riviera got a glimpse of that one time just before they exploded." Admiral Baker sighed. "Those are nice looking ships."

Colonel Townsley was about to say something when the red airlock warning light began to flash indicating the outer door was being opened.

"Steady, Tom," Admiral Baker said softly, clutched the nearest handrail and straightened his stance.

After the normal few minutes the red airlock warning light went out and the steady green light winked on indicating the airlock was pressurized to match the stations pressure. It was another few minutes before the latches withdrew and the door swung toward them.

The tall, trim man wearing a polished blue-black body suit with accomplishment ribbons, braids, ropes and service stars, drifted through the hatchway with the poise of someone accustomed to weightlessness, and looked straight at Admiral Baker. With a crisp salute, Stran came forward.

"Admiral Baker, I presume," he said and extended his right hand. When the Admiral reciprocated he added, "I am Colonel Stran Geaardt of the Galactic Peace Force."

"Very pleased to meet you, Colonel," Admiral Baker replied. "This is my Station Watch Commander, Colonel Townsley."

Stran extended his hand and shook his. "Pleased." Then he turned to the airlock. "I would like to present Captain Jim Woods of your U.S. Air Force," as Jim drifted forward with less poise than Stran had shown, saluted both and shook their hands.

Stran continued, "Chief Warrant Officer Kiile of the Peace Force Marines."

Kiile approached with practiced poise, saluted and shook their hands, and Stran continued, "And Lieutenant Casi Geaardt, also of the Peace Force."

Casi, in her form fitting, polished dress Blue body suit with her ribbons, braids, ropes and stars, drifted gracefully into the chamber. Both Admiral Baker and Colonel Townsley were taken aback a moment before they returned her salute and shook her hand.

Kiile turned back to the airlock. "Twelve, you will remain here and watch over our suits and equipment." Then he turned back as the marine took a stance in front of the open hatch.

"Admiral," Stran said in a soft voice. "I believe we have things to discuss. Please lead the way."

▲

As the admiral led the entourage into the central core and out to his offices in the middle ring, Stran noted they did not meet any other personnel. *'There are others near, but the admiral is keeping them from being seen by us, or us by them.'*

'He's still apprehensive. There are three armed marines ahead of us and three behind us,' Casi summarized.

They followed the admiral into his anteroom where Lieutenant Wardly stood at rigid Attention as they entered. "Lieutenant Anne Wardly," the admiral said, introducing her to the group. "This is Colonel Geaardt, Lieutenant Geaardt, Captain Woods and Chief Warrant Officer Kyle. This way please." Anne followed as he led them into his office where four people waited on the far side of twelve chairs arranged in a wide circle, facing inward.

"May I present," Admiral Baker continued, "Lieutenant Riviera of Surveillance, Sergeant Tillots of Tracking and Navigation, Captain Nesbit of Weapons and Chief Ross of Station Maintenance?"

"Admiral, before we begin," Stran said. "Please understand we are not here as a threat to you. Quite the opposite I assure you. I'd like to introduce my team to you.

"My Campaign Lieutenant Major Kooich and his Wing Second Major Mooren are with me, parked outside keeping an eye on eight unfriendly targets parked in high orbit. Major Kooich and Major Mooren were the two fighters that destroyed the rogue battlecruiser on the twentieth of October. The one that arrived just before your station's computer system was breached from planetside.

"Major Kooich and myself were the two that destroyed the seven fighters you witnessed on the nineteenth of November.

129

Four of my ships under Major Kooich's command destroyed the three battlecruisers you witnessed on the twenty-second of November. Lieutenant Geaardt," he nodded to Casi, "is the pilot that destroyed the five fighters you witnessed on the twenty-third of November over the eastern U.S. Lieutenant Geaardt and Major Mooren destroyed the two fighters that were flanking your station on the twenty-fourth of November. I believe you recorded that event close up. And Lieutenant Geaardt is the pilot that destroyed two battlecruisers and a number of fighters in high orbit that you witnessed on the thirtieth of November."

"Sixty smaller targets," Lieutenant Riviera said softly, "I believe, sir."

Stran nodded and Admiral Baker stared at him and Casi for a long moment before a smile slowly crossed his face. "I think we owe you many thanks."

"Thank you, sir," Stran continued, "but it is part of our job. We are not here to seek accolades for our efforts, but I offer the information to help you understand our loyalties. We have a much larger issue confronting us, and you.

"This is the first time the Peace Force has allowed any of its agents or fighters to willingly show themselves to those outside of our ranks so I wish to make the most of this opportunity."

"I can understand why," the admiral said gesturing to the chairs. "The sudden arrival of those beautiful ships, appearing out of seemingly empty space, could be unnerving to almost anyone. Please make yourselves comfortable."

"One thing before we do, sir," Casi said. "Please have your armed escort either join us or disband."

The admiral stared at her, surprised.

"Please don't feign surprise, sir. You have three armed marines in each of the compartments on either side of your offices," she continued. "They escorted us from the shuttle airlock. They are welcome to keep their weapons and join us, since all of us, each of you included are armed."

Colonel Townsley's face went ashen.

"Colonel," Casi said looking directly at him, "since you arranged their presence, would you please convey our wishes? I do not want a misunderstanding in the conversation to mistakenly degrade into a test of who has the most lethal firepower or who is the quickest to use it."

When Colonel Townsley had gone, Stran turned to Lieutenant Riviera. "Lieutenant, the promotion was long overdue. Congratulations. You have shown a great ability to interpret your sightings with more than reasonable accuracy. Your intuitiveness serves you and your service well."

Surprised, she looked at the admiral, her expression questioning. When he offered no explanation, she simply turned back to Stran and said, "Thank you, sir."

Colonel Townsley returned with the six marines following. He gestured they take positions along the wall beside the admiral's desk, and then he gestured to the chairs and asked that everyone be seated. "Colonel Geaardt, please take a seat where you can see the entry and everyone in the room."

As they found places with Stran's entourage facing the admiral's, Stran decided to stand behind his empty chair and Casi, and likewise the admiral stood behind his empty chair and Lieutenant Wardly.

"Admiral," Stran began, "as you know there is a war going on that has unfortunately sucked you, your staff and your planet in. More correctly, I will say our planet as well, since Captain Woods, Lieutenant Geaardt and myself were born and raised here in the States.

"To continue, there is an organization that consists of many businesses, which has legitimately provided essential needs, products and services to the inhabited systems of the galaxy for many of your centuries. But in the last hundred terran years or so, an arm of those businesses have come under suspicion of illicit trading, black market goods and slaves from many different sources. In the last fifty terran years we have seen an increasing number of terran humans appearing in many marketplaces.

"We are officers in an organization named the Galactic Peace Force, charged with maintaining a peace and right conduct within those inhabited systems. We could be called police officers, peace keepers in a military service, or any number of similar titles. My team began small, as undercover work tends to force one's size to be. One of my original team is piloting a fighter above us, and two," he nodded to Kiile and Jim, "are here with us now. We followed clues for three years, knowing the Traders were here and finally we discovered the slave traders' secluded launch facility, the place where they were shipping their collections from. On the night of twenty-two October and the following morning, my slightly expanded team captured that facility and temporarily stopped their ability to continue shipments."

"Was it a large facility?" the admiral asked.

"It can handle freighters up to five hundred feet in length," Stran answered. "Not as large as the battlecruiser but large enough to ship a couple hundred captives at a time."

"You captured the facility in one night?" Colonel Townsley asked.

"Yes," Stran answered without going into the details that he only had an attack group of six. "The reason I had Captain Woods ask for a meeting is that I have been charged with taking the fight to the source. That includes going off world." Then he turned to Casi. "But Lieutenant Geaardt, with her incredible knack of discovery, has located their second launch facility at a time when I must extend my fight beyond this planet, and without some changes, I will not be able to adequately protect you and stop any ships that try to arrive at the new facility."

"How do you mean 'protect us?'" Colonel Townsley said and instantly caught Admiral Baker's glare.

Stran smiled at the exchange. "Colonel, please understand, I 'am' protecting you. I have maintained an escort in formation with you for over a month and will continue to do so as long as I am able. But with the continued arrivals, like the group we are watching now," he gestured beyond the outer wall, "the escorts may not be enough when I take the bulk of my fighters to a distant fight, thus my offer to implement some changes to help your station."

Suddenly the admiral felt very vulnerable.

"Admiral," Stran continued as if he did not sense the change in mood. "I would like your permission for Chief Warrant Officer Kiile to work with your Chief Ross to install some of our equipment on your station. These systems can be controlled by station personnel of your choosing and will be independently powered. They are systems you are not familiar with and your people will not understand how they work, but they will be useful to you and the station.

"I would like Chief Warrant Officer Kiile to implement two quad laser cannon turrets and a shield generator along with their independent power sources." Stran hesitated and let the admiral consider his words. "The cannons are long range weapons and as Lieutenant Geaardt has proven, they have enough fire power to cut a battlecruiser in half." *'Sorry Bren. I don't mean to keep using you as an example.'*

'It's okay, love,' Casi said and glanced at him with a guarded smile.

"And the Shield Generator," he continued, "will give the station protection during an attack."

"Shields?" Colonel Townsley asked, a smile slowly crossing his face. "Like 'force fields' and 'deflectors' in science fiction cinema and novels?"

Stran stiffened and stared directly at the colonel. "Similar in description, but significantly more sophisticated in actuality."

The admiral's glare at Townsley slowly softened as the colonel realized the import of Colonel Geaardt's offer.

"When active," Stran continued, "this protective barrier will keep everything without specific authorization from penetrating. Of course, it has limits on how much energy it can repel or deflect, but the important thing is it can keep the station from being damaged by incoming objects, even the ion drive emissions of a passing freighter."

Colonel Townsley went pale and slowly smiled at the recalled memories of the near collision of thirty September.

"Colonel Geaardt?" Colonel Townsley finally asked. "Who will train our personnel to use this equipment?"

"Chief Warrant Officer Kiile and one of his marines will provide that service," Stran replied. "You will need to create a closed group of personnel to learn and operate the equipment. Using your existing scanner capabilities with our modifications, your group will be able to defend yourself against significant opposing forces. With the long range cannons, you will be able to engage an enemy before it is close enough to be a serious threat. And with the shield generator, you will be able to block any return fire. I suggest your new group be completely independent of your normal staff and their responsibilities. You will need to maintain secrecy."

Admiral Baker nodded and pondered Stran's comment.

"Sir?" Lieutenant Riviera asked. "Our scanners do not plot some targets all of the time. Sometimes they disappear from the screens while I'm tracking them."

"Lieutenant," Stran said softly, "the solution to that problem is complicated. I cannot give you any equipment that can remedy that occurrence, but I have trained my crews in a way to make the targets visible more often and possibly for longer periods of time. When we make them visible, your scanners will see them also."

"Thank you, sir," she said.

"If the admiral accepts this implementation, someone on your team," he glanced at the seated group, "I suspect Sergeant Tillots or someone like him, will be able to communicate with your unseen escorts or with myself or Major Kooich."

"Sir," Captain Woods said to the admiral. "My group in QCC has purged the moles that were planted by the Traders to aid the takeover of S.S. QuickSilver, and we are now able to maintain secure communications with both you and with the colonel. The colonel is offering you an increased level of safety, especially if the Traders' fighters decide to take action against you and a means to communicate directly with him and his forces. You are still as much of a threat to the new launch facility as you were to the one we captured in October."

"Those are the three things I can offer you," Stran concluded, "until we can push the slave traders from this sector of the galaxy. Other capabilities that we have, I cannot pass on to you without risking our discovery and possibly placing you in very awkward situations with your counter-parts below. Beyond these things that I have offered, I can only provide our continued escorts, advice and possibly answer some of your questions."

Admiral Baker studied the man before him and then smiled. "Colonel Geaardt, I greatly appreciate your asking for this meeting and for you and your staff for coming to explain your wishes. But if I may ask, what do you expect in return? You have defended us in the past and come to offer us help beyond our most ambitious dreams and yet there seems to be little we can provide in return."

"What we are offering will not bring you peace, but will cause you some problems," Stran admitted with a wry smile. "Someone, even some on your station crew, may ask questions when these systems are used. You will not be able to explain what the systems are without creating more questions. Since they have no knowledge of the systems you would describe, they will not believe your explanations and they will not accept your story as to how you came to have the equipment installed on your station."

"Yes," Admiral Baker admitted. "There will be questions."

"I also must warn you," Stran added, again in a lower voice, "the systems will self destruct if anyone tampers with them in any way, tries to open the sealed outer shells, or tries to move them for any reason, like disassembly at a later time or different place. If one of your maintenance personnel, or anyone for that matter, gets too curious, these temporary gifts will become useless chunks of sintered carbon."

'*The Traders' fighters have started a slow descent.*' Casi said softly in Stran's mind. '*STSX says we have approximately half an hour, maybe less before they enter the atmosphere.*'

'*Thanks. Have Major Kooich bring up one of the reserve ships for escort and for him and his four to cloak and depart to intercept and destroy. The new escort will get here before we leave. STSX is already on Alert.*'

Stran looked at the admiral and waited as if his conversation with Casi had not happened.

"As to your question, Admiral," Stran continued when the admiral did not say anything more, "about what I want in return. I want your support in keeping our presence and your knowledge of these new capabilities a secret. We have a common purpose. Right now, the Traders may suspect the Peace Force is interfering with their operations. They do not know for sure and I want to keep it that way as long as I can."

"What would happen if they knew?" Lieutenant Riviera asked when the admiral remained silent.

"They would know they needed to increase the stakes," Stran said, "and that would mean they would bring attack forces. So far they have been trying to remain undetected, to keep their presence secret, to quietly investigate the loss of their launch facility and the loss of their main control center and the disappearance of their key contact on the planet. With one exception, they have been searching for information in a low-key manner, but that may change anyway because in a few minutes they are going to lose their first resupply ship sent since their launch facility fell."

Then he looked back at the admiral. "We will leave you to think about my offer. When you have decided whether you would like the systems installed and who you will have manage their capabilities, contact Captain Woods through QCC. If you wish to have the systems installed, tell him you are waiting on parts and Chief Warrant Officer Kiile will contact you through your private communications link."

Stran stepped back and his three stood.

136

"Thank you Colonel," Admiral Baker said, "for coming and giving me much to consider. I will give you an answer before the end of the week."

"Thank you, sir," Stran said and shook his hand.

The admiral and each of his team shook hands with Casi, Kiile and Jim before the admiral led the way back into the corridor and to the spoke back to the core.

⋀ ⋀ ⋀ ⋀ ⋀

To one side in Obscure's main launch bay, Marine Corporal Sixteen ran Jill and Rose through a series of upper body exercises and Nick and Doug through a series of one-on-one challenges in their first hour and a half of their workout. As soon as their rest and water break was over, he pit Rose against Nick in a series of defensive moves.

Nick was reluctant to engage in a fight with Rose, even if it was semi-real, and she stomped him in each challenge.

"Nick!" Sixteen shouted. "Again! You have to be aggressive. Rose is not learning anything if you do not challenge her. This is not polite company."

After four more challenges, Nick threw Rose and instantly went to help her up.

Sixteen shook his head and made them withdraw. "Doug," he said and then pointed at Jill. "On the mat."

Jill remembered the previous training Twelve had given her and Rose before the attack on Ahaar's Complex and the moves she had used when they went after the man that shot Wally. She knew Doug didn't have those memories, but she also knew Doug was a high school and college wrestler. He had moves she would have to watch out for. And he outweighed her by seventy pounds or more. With Sixteen's signal Doug sprang, instantly going for a neck hold, but Jill dropped, spun under him and came up, slamming her fist down across the back of his neck. When he sprawled head first, she was on him and wrenched his arm up behind him.

In the second challenge, Doug swept her legs out from under her and tried to pin her, but she curled her legs and pushed, flipping him on his back. Up on her feet, she caught one arm, pulled and twisted, rolling him over and wrenched it up behind his back.

The third was no contest. Jill copied Shara's neck grab and slammed him face down when he sprang. With another crack to the back of his neck, Doug spread his arms out and surrendered.

"Damn, Jill!" he said as he rolled over. "It's supposed to be practice."

"Sorry Doug," she said and helped him up. "Shar told me it's never practice. Threats come from unexpected places and at unexpected times. She told me you can always apologize later."

"Well," Doug said, looking at Nick and Rose, "you do fight for real."

Sixteen stepped up and slapped Jill's back. "She's right you know, Doug," he said and glanced at Nick and Rose. "Both Rose and Jill have an advantage. They are remembering what they had to do in actual hand-to-hand combat." He looked at Nick. "I understand you and the colonel were very successful in the attack on this facility."

"Yes, sir," Nick agreed, "but with weapons. We didn't have any hand-to-hand fighting. And we didn't fight women."

"How do you know?" Sixteen asked with a blank stare. "I understand that you didn't engage in hand-to-hand fighting, but there were a significant number of female troopers billeted here. Many in security and I believe your fighting was mainly against security."

Nick's face went ashen.

"Nick," Sixteen said firmly. "You MUST get gender out of your mind. Whether your adversary is male of female is unimportant when they are trying to kill you! Do not be distracted by those details. It WILL be your downfall. And it could cost your teammates their lives."

"Doug," Sixteen turned to him and let Nick digest what he had said. "Your attack on Jill was basically good, but you looked like you expected her to act like one of your wrestling opponents. She is quick, agile and smart. You have to be prepared for that.

"Like Nick, I know you did not get exposed to hand-to-hand fighting, but it is a real part of your survival. You must ALWAYS fight like your life depends on it. You must learn to see quick, think quick, and react quick. You have to fight as if you are the only one that can, as if everything depends on you winning. And remember, you may have to face someone that you once thought was your friend."

Doug's deep breaths were slowing and he nodded, hearing Sixteen's words.

"Yeah," Nick said softly and Sixteen turned with a question in his expression. "The colonel confronted and had to kill his own brother when we attacked this facility. Whether he had any regrets, I don't know, but he fought like Hew, known to us as Howard, was just another enemy soldier shooting at him and Hew was trying to kill him."

Sixteen waited a short moment, then he said, "To the ropes." He gestured to the four ropes reaching from the floor to a gantry arm just below the launch bay's closed portal. "All the way to the top and back down. On the double!"

⋏

Jill had just reached the floor, a couple of seconds ahead of Doug, when she saw Major Glean and Debira sprint from a door on the north side of the launch bay and dart into the corridor of steps that led to the portal hatchway and the Q-Ships outside.

Sixteen noted their times and did not turn at the sound of running feet.

'Shar? What's happening?' Jill asked in her mind. *'LTVC21 is launching in a scramble.'* She turned and absently looked up at the closed launch bay portal and tried to listen to the space

beyond.

After a short moment, Shara answered, *'Can't talk right now. The fighters are descending and Major Kooich is taking his group to intercept.'*

Jill's hand quickly covered her mouth and Nick asked what was wrong. Jill explained what little she knew and that she would listen for more news.

Unaware of Jill's conversation or news, Sixteen looked up from his notepad and said, "Half an hour break. Go to the Mess and relax and then we will start again."

▲ ▲ ▲ ▲ ▲

Once the red airlock warning light began to flash, Colonel Townsley relaxed, glanced out of the wide window and looked at the sleek ship still poised broadside before them. He glanced around and noticed the other ships were gone. He looked high and then out of other windows and realized they were not there, or at least 'not visible' he corrected himself.

He looked back at the colonel's ship in time to see its image waver and quickly fade into transparency and disappear.

When he looked back, Admiral Baker was entering the floor portal to the central tube on his way back to his office. Quickly, Colonel Townsley followed and caught up as they entered the spoke to the middle ring.

"Admiral," Colonel Townsley began as they took the tube outward, "how did the colonel know about Lieutenant Riviera's surveillance and the marines I had following us?"

Admiral Baker shook his head slowly. "I don't know Tom, but they have obviously been watching and studying our routines for quite a while. Whether I like it or not, it is the mark of a good soldier."

"Yes, sir. It is," Colonel Townsley admitted. "It's just spooky the way they seem to know things."

Admiral Baker led the way into his office and asked Anne

to join them. The other four were still there, waiting his return.

"Lieutenant Riviera," the admiral said as he took one of the empty chairs and gestured for everyone to take a seat as well. "Your assessment please."

"Sir," Lieutenant Riviera said. "The colonel did know we had seen each of the encounters he noted, which means he, or his staff, are aware of what we see and do. In a way, I feel good that they are not trying to hide or discredit that knowledge.

"I am also a little intimidated by their apparent combat capability. We know we only saw the two fighters take on and destroy that battlecruiser, but I was completely taken aback to realize that Lieutenant Geaardt accumulated sixty-two kills in one encounter and five in another, that we know of. And that she was right here, just outside when she took down one of the two fighters that we discovered were flanking us."

"Yes. I agree she has shown great capability, Lieutenant," the admiral said, "but what do you think of the colonel's offer?"

"Independent defensive power," she admitted, "is nothing to discard lightly. It completely eliminates the issues we had with defense when our computer system was hacked. You will have to assign Captain Nesbit or someone from Weapons, to manage them, but I think it's a great asset. I don't know how any of this affects Surveillance, but independent fire power and the ability to shield ourselves from return fire is definitely a plus in my book."

Admiral Baker nodded in agreement. "Tillots? Anything to add?"

"No sir," he replied. "I agree with the Lieutenant. Especially if the colonel has to spread his fighter coverage and leave us with a little less of their active protection."

The admiral nodded. "Ross?"

"My only question, sir," Chief Ross smiled, "is how soon can we get them installed and operational."

"Nesbit?"

"The offer sounds good to me," he replied. "It would feel

very good to have 'independent' capability."

"I see you have all bought into our allies and are happy with their offer for continued help," the admiral said. "And Colonel? Any further suspicions?"

"It always pays to be a little leery," Colonel Townsley said, "but at this moment, no. I don't have anything negative to interject."

Admiral Baker slowly pushed himself up out of the chair. "I thank you for your time today. I will consider your comments and let you know what I decide."

With that, Sergeant Tillots led the group out of the office. Lieutenant Riviera lagged a little behind and stopped at Anne's desk when the admiral's door closed.

"Lieutenant Wardly?" she asked. "What do you think of all of this?"

"It's Anne, Lieutenant," Anne said. "But I don't really know what to say. It's all so... so overwhelming. To actually meet people from off world, that can operate off world, to meet the stuff of your shadows."

"It's Jen. Short for Jennifer," Lieutenant Riviera said. "And I agree. I was just looking for another woman's take on all of this. I don't want to sound too 'female' when I talk with the Admiral."

"Thanks, Jen," Anne said. "Speak from your training and knowledge and you won't have a problem with the Admiral."

"Thanks," Jen said and started to turn, but stopped. "Was it me, or could you 'feel' the power and confidence in them, their colonel and especially the lieutenant. It took me by surprise when they walked into the office, especially her."

"Yes," Anne admitted. "I certainly did."

Eighty-Four

"Major Mooren," Major Kooich said into his boom mic, "As the transport approaches, position yourself to cut open the belly section just behind the cockpit. That will disable most of the ship's internal controls and communications. Major Miiles, position yourself to do the same on the topside just behind the cockpit area. A serious, penetrating cut across the back will disrupt the weapons control systems."

"Will do," Major Mooren's voice answered. "TTYF indicates five minutes to engagement."

"We're on it," Lieutenant Miiles confirmed.

"Apache Patrol Two and Three," Major Kooich continued. "Keep your Shield up Full, Cloaked and Sensor blocked. Remember your training, fire and move quickly. Pick a new firing position and then repeat."

"Apache Two understands," Cheral's voice answered.

"Apache Three understands," Ani confirmed.

"Apache Two and Three. You will engage the fighters," Major Kooich added. "KKLC will fly cover and assist where needed. Four minutes. Pick your targets and begin closure. Be smart." Then he spoke into the cockpit, "Light them up, Leeana. Do you have the transport?"

"Yes," she replied. "STSX has given us a target. It's clear enough to actually see details."

"Good," he smiled, "Broadcast the Kyddellan IFF that Kiile gave us, drop visual cloaking and tell the transport to stop their descent or they will be fired upon." Then to his fighters, "Two minutes. Start your runs."

"They see us," Leeana said, "Transmissions jammed. Looks

143

like they're increasing their descent rate."

The patrol fighters rose to meet the descending escort fighters, letting the transport slip past to the waiting Q-Ships. Apache Patrol Two made the first strike and the first, unsuspecting fighter disappeared in a flash of fire and smoke. Apache Patrol Three got the second fighter and Apache Patrol Two jumped on the third.

The transport returned fire, aiming at the points where the fighters were when they fired. Apache Patrol Three cursed softly as a shot caught her shields and tossed the fighter aside. TTYF8 waited patiently and caught the belly of the transport as it passed, disrupting its maneuvering controls. Suddenly the transport coalesced when the communications center and the control centers failed; KVWC33 pounced.

Leeana watched the scanner's blips and targets, offering muttered encouragements as they seemed to dart about with random abandon.

"TTYF and KVWC," Major Kooich said softly. "Go for the kill."

He watched the blossoms erupt across the transports back and belly as a side hatch began to open. "They're opening a hangar bay," Leeana said with more urgency than she intended.

"We've got them," Cheral's voice answered and the two patrol fighters darted for the opening, filling it with cannon fire.

Apache Patrol Two caught three fighters as they tried to launch and Patrol Three caught two before KVWC33's cannon cut the hangar bay open in a huge fireball and boiling smoke. TTYF8 focused on the area just forward of the engines as the transport began to roll.

"Pull back," Major Miiles said as the forward section of the transport separated and slowly fell aside trailing smoking debris.

In the next seconds, the remaining bulk of the ruptured hull began to burn fiercely and culminated in a rapidly expanding explosion. The engines and fuel cells erupted a second later and fiery smoke boiled around the fragments and slowly dissipated along the freighter's descending flight path.

"Apache Patrol Two and Three. Two fighters left," Leeana said as Patrol Two swung around and finished one of them.

"Can you get it Ani?" Cheral asked as she lined up on the second just as it disappeared.

"Yeah," Ani said softly as the blossom dissolved into nothingness.

A moment passed silently before Major Kooich asked, "Damage report."

"Patrol Two is okay."

"Patrol Three is okay."

"TTYF8 is okay," Major Mooren said softly.

"KVWC33 is okay."

"Join up," Major Kooich said. "One slow pass to be sure the area is clear and then we can stand down."

He led the flight around the near space, noting the few remnants and decided they were small enough to ignore. They would either drift away or eventually settle and burn up harmlessly in the atmosphere.

"Stran has left the station," Leeana said to Major Kooich. "STSX says 'Well Done' and suggests we return to base."

"Apache Flight," Major Kooich said into his boom mic. "Well done. Compliments from the commander as well. Formation landing at Obscure please. Debrief will be at the ranch in one hour plus thirty. Casual dress."

⚠ ⚠ ⚠ ⚠ ⚠

Dave Barns munched on peanuts and sipped his beer in Patty's Pub, a half block off Main in Clay. Don Nikle doodled absently on a napkin.

"Not a sound, huh?" Don asked as if he hadn't heard Dave clearly. "No signals from the tracking modules? Nothing?"

"That is what I hear. Abe said he planted a transmitter and a tracking module on each patrol car and two transmitters on the marshal's office windows."

"So now what?" Don asked and took a sip of his beer.

"Abe is going to check the cars again tonight," Dave said. "And if the modules are gone, bounced off or something, he will install new ones. He suspects he did not get the grime cleaned off good enough for them to stick. He knows one is working, but it has not moved since he interrogated its signal."

"He will give us a status in the morning?" Don asked, still concerned that all of the units seemed to have failed. "We must know what the new marshal and deputies are thinking and doing."

"Yes. In the morning after everyone is on duty."

Don studied his doodles for a moment. "Have any of the Council members come up with names for possible new Elders?" he finally asked. "It has been a month since Malcolm and Charley disappeared when Ahaar's last freighter exploded. Then the next day, Harry Woods and Harold Danley disappeared."

"The answer is 'no,' and it was two weeks before that when Harold said the judge died or was captured."

"That was strange," Don said, glancing around their corner table to be sure no one was close enough to hear them. "Harold said the judge fell into that ravine and he just fled, ran away."

"He did say there were six people that confronted them," Dave said, justifying Harold's actions. "He could not fend them off and go after the judge at the same time."

"I suppose," Don admitted. "But he said both the Smallwood and the Thomas women were there." He thought a moment. "Has anyone seen either of them around town?"

"Not that I know of. Some of the kids from the college that we use, checked on Jill Thomas' place and said it didn't look like anyone had come or gone in a couple of months."

"They could be out at the Smallwood ranch," Don surmised.

"That is possible. Harry sent some people to check on the ranch before he disappeared, but I never heard if they found anything."

"There also have not been any further demands from Ahaar," Don said, "concerning the movement of the Reeds families. I checked Harry's phone terminal at his place in Hawthorne. Ahaar tried to call him just after the incident with the last freighter, just after Harry and Harold disappeared. Nothing after that."

"So we do not know if Ahaar still has need of the two women."

"No, we do not," Dave admitted. "Nor could we deliver them if we had them. I tried to find Ahaar's communications number in Harry's things, but nothing. I have no way to reach him and be sure we are not in breach of some agreement Harry or the judge might have made."

"I am assuming he will contact one of us or leave a message on Harry's console if he needs us to do something."

"Maybe," Don said, his mind still considering the puzzling aspect of his dilemma.

▲ ▲ ▲ ▲ ▲

Shara double checked the arrangement of the chairs in the formal portion of the living room. Matti and Cara strived to position the chairs so everyone could see the fireplace where Greg usually stood to address the meetings he called. The group planned for today was smaller than some they had before, but the arrangement needed to place the majors in front of the others and ensure they had a clear view.

'You might have to speak more from the center of the room, love,' she said as Greg came out of the hallway from their bedroom.

'That's okay,' he replied silently as he stopped beside her and placed his arm around her shoulders. "I'm thinking we're

twelve? Four Q-Ships with two apiece, two cadets, Kiile and Jim."

"Fourteen if Captain Iims and Cadet Moss come," she added.

Greg looked at her. "They weren't participants, so I didn't invite them."

"Well," she said, looking back at him with her 'you should have' look. "Captain Iims may want to listen so he knows what training he needs to focus on in the future."

Greg smiled. "I suppose." Then he said *'STSX, please include Captain Iims and Cadet Moss in my debriefing invitation.'*

⚖

At the appointed time, nearly everyone descended upon the ranch. Nick, Jill, Doug and Rose were early and waited until everyone had arrived and were seated before they took places at the dining room table. Greg placed Major Kooich and Leeana on the loveseat, Major Mooren and Franni on the long couch and Major Miiles and Meecia in the overstuffed chairs arranged at the end of the loveseat. Kiile, Jim, Cheral and Cadet Tigs took the front chairs in the formal portion of the living room and Captain Iims and Cadet Moss the chairs behind them.

When everyone had settled, Shara came into the room and took her place in the overstuffed chair beside the fireplace with Greg standing by the hearth beside her.

"Welcome," he said in greeting. "Today has been an interesting day, a first for many of us, in one way or another. To all of you involved, I must again say 'Well done.'"

He paused a moment and glanced around the room, his gaze stopping on each face intently looking back.

"This afternoon was the first time a Shadow has been specifically allowed to openly step forward and expose themselves to an outsider. Four of us, myself, Casi, Squad Leader Kiile and Captain Woods, boarded the space station S.S. QuickSilver for a face to face meeting with its commanding officers." Greg continued and explained the general details behind the meeting and what the Peace Force was offering the station and its crew.

"We will continue to escort the station for its protection, but in the future, they may be better able to defend themselves." He again glanced around the room. "Any questions?"

Cadet Tigs and Lieutenant Meecia Miiles asked for clarification on a couple of points and Greg explained the reasons behind his decisions and the director's agreement. When there were no more questions, he continued. "Major Kooich, will you please present your comments and suggestions on today's engagement with the Trader's supply transport and its fighter escort."

Greg stepped behind Shara as Major Kooich rose and faced the group.

"I only have a few criticisms," he began. "Cadet Tigs, I noticed you took two hits from the transport's cannons. In the future, unless you are in immediate danger, take your time setting up your shots. Then fire and immediately move. Sideways, up, down , backwards. It doesn't matter where, but immediately MOVE! Then you can take your time setting up your shot. I know it is difficult under the circumstances of combat, but you must develop a rhythm and use it for every shot."

"Yes, sir," Cadet Tigs answered. "I will remember."

"Was there any damage to your fighter?" Major Kooich continued and when she shook her head, he moved on. "Captain Haak. When you and Cadet Tigs attacked the hangar bay, you seemed a little too anxious, crowding the space. KVWC33 could have caught you with either a cannon shot of their own or with the explosion they set off. Always pay attention to where and how the others in your group are attacking and remember your cannons are just as effective with a little more separation from the targets."

"Yes, sir," Cheral said with a nod.

"KVWC33," he said, turning to Major Miiles. "I'm wondering if you had trouble acquiring the transport. You did not engage with Major Mooren. You seemed to wait until its cloaking was disabled. Was there a problem?"

"No sir," Major Miiles said. "I was just... out of position when TTYF8 commenced his attack. It won't happen again."

Major Kooich watched him a moment, certain Meecia had said something he did not like while he was speaking. "Anything you wish to add?"

Major Milles shook his head and looked at Meecia.

"Very well," Major Kooich said and glanced at his notepad. "As of today, the credits are as follows,

"KVWC33 has two half kills for a total of one full kill. KVWC33 shared in a battlecruiser kill with TTYF8 on twenty-two November and again today.

"TTYF8 has three half kills and two full kills for a total of three and a half kills. TTYF8 shared in a battlecruiser kill with KKLC14 on twenty-two October and the two shared kills with KVWC33. One fighter kill near the space station on Thanksgiving day, twenty-four November, one drop ship kill on eight December.

"Apache Patrol Three, Cadet Tigs, has made it onto the honors board with six full fighter kills today." The major paused as Cheral, the majors and the rest of the gathering clapped in encouragement.

"And Apache Patrol Two, Captain Haak, has also made the honors board with eight full fighter kills today."

The majors and the cadets again clapped and voiced their encouragement.

"Again Apache Fighter Wing, a very 'well done.' Please review your combat video files and those of the other group members when you have quiet time. Apply these criticisms as constructive in nature and thank you for your support," Major Kooich said and turned to Greg. "Colonel, that is all I have for today's debrief."

"Thank you, Major," Greg said and turned to the group.

Major Mooren shouted, "Attention!" and everyone stood

crisply.

Greg saluted them and when they returned the salute, he said, "At Ease. Please help yourselves to refreshments," and he gestured to the spread on the dining room table that Matti and Cara had laid out, working around Nick, Jill, Doug and Rose. The drinks ranged from beers to non-alcoholic beverages, hot and cold, and the snacks ranged from cheeses to Annie's sweet breads.

When Cadet Tigs stepped into line, Shara leaned close and said softly, "I forgot to duck a few times myself." Then she smiled and added, "I had to get STSX's entire bank of shields repaired afterwards." Cadet Tigs smiled back and Shara could tell she felt much better about Major Kooich's criticism.

Then Shara turned to Cheral and clasped her forearm and said softly, "Very nice, Cousin. I only got five my first time."

When Shara looked up, she saw Greg standing in front of the fireplace watching her with a wide smile and suddenly she wished the house was not full of people.

Tuesday, December 20

"Colonel?" Major Kooich called as Greg and Shara were about to leave through the back door off the dining room. He quickly hurried from the living room to catch him. "Have you heard anything on our next Q-Ships?"

"Yes. Sorry," Greg said as he stopped and turned around. "Most likely Tuesday the twenty-seventh. I was given LLRT12 and KCMM9, but I must admit, I did not check the crew names."

"Leeana can get them," he said then he changed the subject. "I was thinking about sending one of the ships over the new launch facility on a regular basis. Add it to our daily patrols."

"I think that's a good idea," Greg admitted. "But since I brought back four extra remotes, you should have your patrols drop one, leave it there for a full day and exchange it with another the next day. We can have full coverage with only one regular trip each day and we'll respond if something shows up."

"Very good, Colonel," Major Kooich said. "May we use one of those to drop today?"

"Take Ten," he said, "and then exchange it with Nine tomorrow. STSX will send them to Obscure for your use."

"Thanks, Colonel. I'll get the mission assigned," Major Kooich said and went back to talk with Leeana.

▲▲▲▲▲

With the overnight snows in the high plains above Riggs Valley, Wally changed his travel plans and decided on the longer, southern route home. The less scenic, lower elevations across the country south and east of the valley was less enjoyable, but he didn't really relish the thought of possibly spending the day in the north, stranded in a snow bank or digging out from one.

He started from the capital around five in the morning, knowing that in good weather the southern route would take ten hours at best. The trip had begun uneventful and unusually dry for late December, but as the highway skirted around the south side of the 8,226 foot Grey's Peak, the remnants of the last snowfall became more and more evident. It was late morning under the looming overcast sky when he turned north on the state highway that wandered up through Riggs Valley. The Pine forest thickened before he was even with Grey's Peak and the expansive, rolling southern vistas disappeared behind him.

Just above Grants, about half way down the winding slope to the bridge over the Deerskin River, Wally saw an old truck with a camper in its bed parked along the side of the road. As he approached, he could see someone on the passenger side, kneeling beside the truck. He slowed and switched the jeep's flashing rack lights on and stopped behind the truck.

"Hello," he hollered as he got out and walked toward the truck. "Are you having some trouble? Is there anything I can help with?"

The man appeared to be in his forties as he slowly stood up and faced him. A slender woman slipped out of the passenger side door.

"Hello," Wally repeated. "Can I help you?"

The man motioned for Wally to come closer, beside the truck.

"Hi," he said. "Glad to see you."

"You the new Marshal?" the woman asked, gesturing to the emblem on the jeep's hood and the star on his jacket.

"Yes, ma'am," he replied, "Marshall Wally Lima from Riggin. Are you folks having some problems?"

"Might say that," the man said. "Flat tire and a flat spare."

Wally looked at the spare and then at the tire the man had removed from the right front.

"Well, my spare won't fit," he said rubbing his chin, "so how 'bout I take you back to Grants to get them fixed?"

"We were heading up to Riggin," the woman said. "My sister has a place there on the west side of town and asked us to come up."

"Is it just the two of you?" Wally asked and noticed the man's reluctance. Wally continued without making it obvious he noticed. "Grants is close, so why don't I take you and your tires there. Then I can bring you back and get you back on your way. What do ya say?"

The woman nodded and the man slowly acquiesced.

"Name's Thad," he said, "and this is my wife, Betti."

"Nice to meet you," Wally said. "Let me get some gloves and you get your personals gathered up."

Once the tires were loaded in the back, strapped half in and half out, Wally situated Betti in the back seat, Thad in the passenger seat and he got in. The ride to Grants was congenial,

153

with Thad slowly warming up, as he accepted the idea that he was riding in a state police vehicle and was not in trouble. Wally found out they were from a small farmstead quite a ways east of Grants below the lower of the three lakes in the valley, aptly named South Lake. Thad grew some food crops, though not many grew well at this altitude or in this climate, and he raised a few cows and sheep for meat. Betti was a seamstress and did sewing for the locals in the area around their farm and the small town of Community.

When they stopped to have the tires repaired, Thad sent his wife off to get them a bite to eat. Wally declined his offer to join them, saying he had just finished a sandwich before he stopped to help them. While Thad and Betti ate, Wally chatted with the station attendant who pointed out the right front tire could not be repaired as he pushed his finger through the bullet hole in the sidewall.

Wally realized there obviously was more to their reason for traveling than just a holiday visit and he made note to investigate if he could. The thought of their truck left unattended suddenly bothered him, but he knew they would have to wait and face that concern when they got back to it. Wally had the attendant mount a new tire, paid for it and when Thad paid the much lesser amount for patching the spare, they were back on the road north.

Thad and Betti's truck seemed unharmed and Wally was relieved when it started after they finished installing the front tire. Thad wanted to pay Wally for his help, or for the gas or something for his kindness, but Wally refused to accept anything.

"If you'd like," Wally said to Thad through his open, driver's side window, "I'll follow you in to Hawthorne and if everything's okay there, I'll leave you to make the rest of the trip on your own."

Thad agreed and thanked Wally again, and they started north. At Hawthorne, Thad and Betti stopped to refuel their truck and Wally bade them goodbye, and hoped they would have a good journey the rest of the way to Betti's sister's place.

⋏

The ten hour trip had turned into a thirteen hour trip by the time Wally reached his house, and another half before he got everything unloaded and put away. It was nearly seven when he pushed Hap's front door open and recoiled from the loud, pulsating music and the flashing, jittery holographic brewer's signs dancing to the beat of the music. He caught his breath, forced himself forward and found his stool at the end of the bar.

Wally smiled as he noticed that someone had neatly engraved "Marshal Wally Lima" on the stool seat and had a new mug with a marshal's star, turned upside down on a coaster on the counter. He had barely slipped onto the stool when Carole stopped behind the bar.

"Good to see you back," she said, her voice slightly raised to speak over the music. "How was the trip?"

"Very long," he answered and turned his mug over.

Carole quickly filled it with coffee from a fresh carafe.

"Any specials?" he asked. "I'm starved."

Carole told him about the two on the menu and he picked one. When she went to the kitchen pass-through window and keyed his order into her hand unit, Wally slowly scanned the room and noted that the crowd was smaller than he expected. One couple was dancing in the small space opened up by moving two tables to join with others, but mostly the patrons were just occupying booths and a few tables, talking and laughing about one thing or another. When he turned back, Carole was standing at the end of the bar counter, patiently watching him.

"Seems quiet enough," he said and took a sip from his mug.

"The people, yes," Carols said with a smile, "the music, no."

Wally nodded in agreement and Carole turned back to the kitchen and went to get his food. She placed the plate on the counter as he refilled his mug.

"Thanks," he said and started eating.

"When did you eat last?" she asked.

"About nine I think," he said, hesitating to think. "Well, earlier, sometime just after sunrise."

"Well," she stared at him and shook her head, "at least you had something today."

He ate a few more bites and smiled at her. "Not as good as your cooking, but it sure tastes good in a pinch."

Carole made her way around the room, checking on the customers she was serving, refilling cups and getting drink refills as needed. One customer added desert and another pulled two tables together as friends arrived and expanded their party. By the time she got back to check on him, he was finished and had laid his payment on the counter beside the plate and stacked utensils.

"I think I'm going to go and take a shower and get cleaned up," he said as he stood up.

"Will I see you after work?"

"If I'm not here, come by," he said and covered a yawn with his hand. "Actually, come by and if I don't answer when you knock, let yourself in. I'd really like to see you."

"Okay," she said and smiled. "I have the key you gave me. I'll just come by."

He quickly caught her hand, squeezed it gently and then turned to the door.

A

When he got back to his place, he backed the jeep into the garage beside his patrol car and closed the overhead door. The timed living room light was on when he opened the door into the house and he hung his coat on the new rail of pegs he had put up behind the front door. Absently he double checked the other two doors and then checked the windows and blinds.

Satisfied everything was in order he went into his bedroom and turned the master shower on. When he had finished cleaning up and had washed the remains of the day away, he sat down on the edge of his single bed and slipped on a pair of sweat pants and a t-shirt. He thought about having a glass of wine while he waited for Carole to get off work, but he didn't have the energy to go and get it, so he stretched out on the bed thinking he would rest his eyes for just a bit instead.

⅄

Sometime in the night, he moved and woke up enough to realize all of the house lights were off and that Carole lay close beside him with the blanket he usually kept at the foot of his bed spread over both of them. The scent of her, the feel of her warm body stretched out against his with her leg curled and resting on top of his, the sound of her soft breathing, her head resting on his arm and shoulder and her arm stretched across his chest comforted him. He curled his arm around her, closed his eyes and fell quietly back to sleep.

C.3482.373

"Enter," Chairman Sorgat said and looked up as Intelligence Director Kraast and Merchandise Director Korveel walked into the room and stopped at the far end of the conference table. "Come," Chairman Sorgat said as he rose to greet him. "Please take a seat."

The chairman walked around the desk and took a seat at the conference table and turned to face Director Kraast as he sat down with an empty chair between them. Kraast's expression was grim.

"And what grievous news do you bear today?" the chairman asked, almost reluctant to guess as Director Korveel settled uneasily into the chair just beyond Kraast.

"Chairman Sorgat," Director Kraast began, "it is news about your resupply transport." He laid a thin notepad on the table and tapped a sequence. When the image solidified, he turned the pad for the chairman to read. "We have lost contact with them."

The chairman ground his teeth and stared at both directors.

"Sir," Director Kraast continued. "We sent a surveillance

ship to follow them, in the hopes that we could get some information concerning the other disappearances. It was twelve pars behind the transport when it stopped, high above the planet on C.3482.370. It was parked in waiting three pars out when the transport contacted the launch facility and announced they were descending with the intent to land and off load their supplies."

"We have contacted the facility," Director Korveel said, "and have confirmed that neither the transport nor any of its escort fighters made any further contact and that they did not arrive at the facility. I was told the descent should have taken slightly more than half a par, but nothing arrived."

"After we lost contact," Director Kraast added, "our surveillance ship was sent closer to investigate, but it found nothing."

The chairman slowly got up and paced beside the long table. "And what does Intelligence make of all of this?"

"We are becoming very certain that some sort of surveillance system has been established on the planet," Director Kraast said. "It is appropriate to assume all ships and personnel sent to the planet have been cloaked and sensor blocked, since that is normal practice and it is unlikely that all of them disregarded this operating standard. Therefore, we must conclude that whoever is there knows when someone new arrives in orbit, on the surface or just about anywhere else."

"But how can that be on a planet with such a large population?" the chairman asked when Kraast stopped and looked at him.

"We do not know," Director Kraast said. "I am certain there has to be some way, some way we have not tried, to get someone in."

"Director?" Director Korveel asked softly. "Could someone from the new launch facility move about without creating the sense that someone new had arrived?"

The chairman stopped and Director Kraast turned to look at Korveel. "They might. We do not know what form of surveillance system they are using, but you do offer a point worth considering." He looked up at the chairman. "It will not help us get supplies delivered, but it might help them resupply themselves, and maybe they can get to Director Ahaar's complex and get some information on what has happened."

"Director Korveel," the chairman said with the faintest of a smile, "please contact the facility and see if anything can be worked out."

Wednesday, December 21

Coleen was standing on the back patio of their northern Florida home, two suitcases beside her as she waited for her husband, Brendan Cassel, to bring his cases and join her. Casually looking across their large treed lot in the newer residential development near Gainesville, she was anxious to see her son Greg and his new wife Shara again. As unorthodox and complicated as their life was, she was very pleased when Greg took the time and had contacted her and asked them to spend their holidays with them in the snow covered mountains on their ranch.

It was hard for her to believe that it had only been three weeks since Shara had found her and Brendan trapped in the Traders' Virginia complex basement, trapped by her own unthinking folly. She had convinced Brendan to go with her and the three men she thought also were looking for the man behind all of the missing people. Unwittingly, she did not question them until it was too late.

Shara was the one that discovered them and the fact they were held to see if anyone would come looking for them. She smiled, remembering how easily Shara and her two friends, Jill and Rose, had taken command of the situation. Coleen's head still spun when she thought about Shara following the man named Ahaar on a device she called a remote and then the two of them going with Jill and Rose on two remotes to an invisible ship floating above the complex to wait until Shara returned.

The major and lieutenant, good friends of Shara's, explained what had been happening and how taking them aboard kept them safe, unseen and unreachable by any of Ahaar's allies or troopers.

But she sighed, the real surprise came after Shara had returned and during the introductions, when Shara figured out the relationships and introduced her to her husband, the commander of the operation and a colonel in the Peace Force. When Shara heard Coleen's maiden name was Malone and knowing they had Peace Force tags, she put the pieces together from the stories Greg had told her. Shara had explained that Greg had taken his mother's maiden name for his own when she was capture by slavers and he was ten. Then Shara introduced herself as Shara Malone and her husband as Greg Malone, her lost son.

She turned as the French door behind her opened and Brendan stepped out and sat his two cases beside hers. "I sure hope they have room for all of this," he said. "I know they have a good sized ship, but I don't remember a luggage compartment."

"We'll manage," she said and caressed his cheek. "Shara says they're a couple of minutes out." Coleen looked up and searched the bright morning sky.

"They must have gotten an early start," Brendan said thinking about the time difference and saw her looking. "You won't see them coming."

"Maybe an early start," Coleen agreed, "but it doesn't take them long to get some place."

"True," Brendan said and noticed Coleen's change in expression.

"They're here," she said with an edge of excitement in her voice.

Just off the patio, she caught the change in the view and Greg seemed to solidify out of thin air. He stepped forward and hugged his mother as Shara and Jim Woods coalesced behind him.

Shara quickly hugged Brendan and then Coleen when Greg released her and turned to shake Brendan's hand. Jim stepped forward and shook hands with both of them.

"Don't mind me," Jim said with a smile. "I'm just helping as a bell boy until we get to Lynchburg. Are there more bags or is this it?"

"No," Coleen said, "I think this is all."

"Okay," Jim said as he tied a cord through all of the handles, "I'll get them loaded and we'll be off when you're ready. Six, over here." Then he tied the cord to Six's second stirrup, and mounted the first. He activated his veil, lifted the cases to STSX and placed them inside.

"He makes that look easy," Brendan said, turning at the sound of the doorbell. "I wonder who..."

"It's a neighbor, Brendan," Shara said, relaying STSX's identification.

"We're not home, dear," Coleen said and caught Brendan's hand. "Let's not delay Greg and Shara."

⅄

The neighbor rang the bell a second time and when no one answered, he turned and cut across the lawn, headed to the next house. Part way across the side yard, he heard multiple voices coming from their back yard and he stopped and back tracked, following the almost distinguishable words, but when he turned around the back corner of the house, no one was there.

He glanced around and looked at the closed back door, wondering if the speakers had gone inside. He knocked, but still no one came and reluctantly he turned back and crossed the yard to the next house. He was almost there when he heard the soft chatter again and turned, absently looking up into the bright, clear sky.

Eighty-Five

Wally, still in his sweat pants and t-shirt had the coffee made and the carafe filled by the time Carole came out of the main bath and stopped at the end of the kitchen counter. Wally turned, set the carafe and two mugs on the counter and chuckled. He kissed her and said, "Good morning, for a second time. We match, except for the bagginess."

She looked down and pulled at the loose t-shirt. "I wasn't sure if you'd mind, but I rummaged around and found a shirt and another pair of your sweat pants last night."

"I certainly don't mind," he said as he filled the mugs. "You look great in my sweats, baggy and all. Are you hungry yet?"

He handed her a mug and she nodded over a sip. "What've you got to fix?"

"Most anything for a regular breakfast, or..." he paused as he checked the refrigerator, "I can do biscuits and gravy, pancakes, waffles, crepes with fruit filling, fruit salad with a limited selection of fruits, cinnamon rolls, fruit tarts... About anything you want." He stopped and looked at her over the open refrigerator door. "After finding you here last night and realizing you hadn't just found me asleep and gone home," he said, trying to express his feelings, "I'll fix you about anything you want."

She set her mug down, pulled the baggy pant legs up, walked over to him and pushed the refrigerator door closed. When he leaned down to her, she wrapped her arms around his neck and he straightened up, holding her tight as she wrapped her legs around him.

⋏

After Wally followed Carole back to her place, she cleaned up and got ready for work. He drove them over to Dan's new home on Oak, just east of Hurt, in the second block north of the elementary and high school campus. He noted Ted and Thom's patrol cars parked by the curb just north of the corner beside the house with the rented moving van backed in the driveway and open to the double car garage. Wally stopped along the curb on Oak and helped Carole out.

"Hello," Wally called as they entered the garage. Thom and Ted's faces appeared in the doorway into the house. Wally noticed the van was nearly empty.

"In here Wally," Dan's voice carried from inside and he quickly joined the other two in the doorway. "Hi Carole. Come in, come in."

Wally followed Carole through the door into the large dining room and he saw Dan hurry into a hallway. Moments later Dan came back with a pretty, slender woman in tow.

"Mandy," he said as he stopped in the dining room, "This is Wally Lima and Carole Davis." Then he turned to her, "Wally, Carole, this is my wife Mandy. And oh," he continued when a young red-headed girl in jeans and a bright yellow top hurried up the hall to see what was happening, "our daughter Blaire. She's seven going on seventeen."

Wally greeted Mandy and bent low to say "hello" to Blaire. Carole followed Wally's lead and greeted them. "Mandy," Carole said as she straightened up from greeting Blaire and handed her a small handled bag. "Some body and hand lotions and special soaps to help you adjust to our winters. I hope you like them."

"Thanks Carole," Mandy said. "These will be greatly appreciated, I'm sure. Do you live close by?"

"Yes," Carole said, "Across Main on Hickory. Riggin is really a small town, very easy to get around. Well, once they plow the streets this time of year. I also work at the college hang out, Hap's Place, five blocks west of here at Main and Oak."

"Wally," Thom called from the garage. "Can you give us a hand?"

"Looks like I'm needed," he said to Carole and then went to

help Thom and Ted.

Mandy led Carole into the living room and Blaire flopped down on the couch.

"I bet you're glad to be here," Carole said to Blaire.

"Yup," she said with a big smile. "I like the snow."

"Well, Blaire," Carole said bending close, "that's good because we get a lot of it."

"We're both glad to be here. I was beginning to think we wouldn't ever be able to live together," Mandy said as she sat down beside Blaire and gestured Carole to the cushioned chair beside a stack of boxes.

"How long has Dan been away?" Carole asked, instantly wondering if she was being too nosy.

"A long time. His assignments haven't been long by themselves, but they've been coming so rapidly." Mandy toyed with Blaire's hair. "Over the last five years he's had twelve assignments and only a few days off in between."

Carole was startled. "Wally said he'd been bouncing around a lot, but I had no idea."

"Maybe this is a good sign," Mandy said with a guarded smile. "This the first time in all of those years he's even considered moving us."

"I hope it is a good sign too," Carole smiled, not certain how much of her and Wally's personal conversations she should mention. She chose to play it safe. "But Wally told me he's going to do all he can to make this a long assignment."

Mandy's smile grew. "Obviously, I'd like that." Then Mandy changed the subject. "Before they call me to tell them where to put things, can I ask you a couple of questions?"

"Sure."

"I know these are silly questions, but Dan says you're a local."

"Yes. Born and raised here," Carole answered and then remembered. "Did Dan remember to tell you that both of you and Blaire are invited to Christmas dinner on Sunday. My folks have invited Wally and all of the deputies, and of course, in your case, their family. I'll get the times to Wally and he can tell everyone."

"That's wonderful," Mandy said. "I'll barely have time to get a small tree and a few decorations up. I hadn't even thought about Christmas dinner."

"Now you don't have to worry about it," Carole said. "My sister will be in town and she has a two, almost three year old. A little young for Blaire maybe, but still someone to play with. Okay, your next question."

"Are you and Wally a couple?" Mandy asked, "Or just friends?"

"Both actually," Carole said, surprised by the question.

"I ask because over the years I've only met one of Dan's many bosses," she explained. "And that one just had girlfriends. Every time I'd get to know one, he'd change and I'd have to get to know another one. It wasn't like we saw them often, but more like each time I saw him, he had a new girlfriend. I can sort of accept that with the deputies, like with Ted and Thom, but with Blaire I was an at home mom and didn't make friends very well. I know I've just met you, but I'm hoping that you might be around to help show me the ropes."

"I see," Carole said. "All I can say is that so far Wally and I seem to be a good fit for each other. At least I'm happy with it. I've only known Wally five or six weeks now, and we've been through a lot together since we met. But if something happens and we don't work out, I'll still be here and you can still call on me for anything."

"Thanks. That's nice of you," Mandy admitted.

Carole glanced at her watch. "Mandy, I'm afraid I have to run or I'll be late for work. I'm off on Sundays and in the mornings until eleven and then I work to midnight. Wally and I haven't decided which day is good for my second day off, so that's still waiting for the horse to come back." She stood up and said "goodbye" to Blaire, and again telling Mandy to call her if she needed anything.

"Wally," she called as she went into the garage and he quickly came around from the front of the house. "I've got to run. I can walk if you're—"

"No way," he said and turned to Thom. "I'll be back after making our rounds to see how you're doing." Then he hurried, helped Carole into the jeep and drove her to Hap's.

C.3482.374

"Do we have an answer from the Rings yet, Tam?" the Q-Ship pilot, Major Fila asked. They had been patiently waiting at an assigned Watcher's point in clear space. Without a specific task, she had her cushioned pilot's chair swiveled to aft facing and had been discussing the few surprises they had in this mission assignment.

"Nothing yet," Nav-Com Lieutenant Tam said as she scanned the message logs again. "We should hear any time now. The launch report said the freighter was coming our way with a load of empty ore shipping containers. But..."

"What did you hear?" Major Fila asked.

"There was a Shadow report that some of the empty ore containers were emitting faint power signatures and further investigation indicated they most likely contain envirocubes."

"That must be why they asked us to wait," Major Fila smiled.

"Message coming in," Tam said and swiveled back to her consoles. "We're downloading a file that originated from Q-STSX1 and Colonel Geaardt. The message says when we suspect cloaked activity to periodically broadcast these codes empathically. Some of the targets may light up on the scanners. There is also a set of codes for body cloaking."

"They say we can light up cloaked targets?" Major Fila repeated in surprise.

"Some cloaked targets, Fila," Tam clarified. "Apparently we have twenty-four large mass codes to try. The message says Colonel Geaardt discovered he could put the cloaking transmitters into a maintenance mode which displays the location of the transmitter and the scanner can pick them up. He was able to grow the list to what we just received. Lieutenant Geaardt, however, is credited for discovering she could put the transmitters in a diagnostic mode which turns cloaking off for a short period of time."

"Always knew that Colonel was something special," Major Fila said softly.

"He has a *mate*, Major," Tam said flatly, recognizing Fila's tone of voice.

"I know. I know," Major Fila said. "Maybe he has a friend." Then she changed the subject and glanced at the chronometer. "Let's try the list of codes and see if you can pick anything up."

"I'm on it," Tam said and turned to the console. The first several broadcasts did not result in any scanner traces, but after nearly a par, a single blip appeared. Lieutenant Tam forced herself to wait another four or five centipars and then broadcast another series.

"Positive! We have one," Tam said, "at the far edge of the scanner. Flight track is consistent with our target's expected track. Oh, ho! I've got four! Looks like the escorts we've heard about."

"Tell the Rings," Major Fila said. "Tell them we're going to follow them and request a patrol cruiser for an intercept and boarding. Give them all the details."

⚔

Three pars after picking up the freighter and its escorts, Lieutenant Tam broke the comfortable silence they shared on these long missions. "Fila, patrol cruiser *Brigstoan* has hailed us. They will join up in about six to ten centipars. They have the target on scanner and ask if we will neutralize the escorts."

"Reply affirmative, with pleasure," Major Fila said and glanced over her shoulder. Tam was aft facing, watching the multiple displays in her consoles.

"Reply sent," Tam acknowledged. "When they are ready to intercept, I'll see if we can disable their cloaking with the 'lieutenant's' trick." She stressed the word 'lieutenant' as a not-so subtle jab at Fila, a reminder of the colonel's personal status. "Too bad you missed the awards ceremony, Fila. His 'lieutenant' is quite beautiful and seems to be extremely talented."

"Yeah, keep rubbing it in," Fila rejoined. "You said she bested the number of standing aerial kills for a cadet, didn't you?"

"Uh-huh," Tam said as she switched one scanner to a long range mode. "Sixty-three, I think. All solo except for one. Now she has her pilot's ribbon and is Q-Ship qualified as well."

"Just my luck, he'd find a real and talented gem," Major Fila chuckled.

After a few more centipars, the communications display chimed. "Message from the patrol cruiser. They are alongside at half a click to our right. The scanner..." she hesitated as she adjusted another scanner display, "...has them. IFF confirmed."

"Tell them we are ready when they are."

"They're ready, Major," Tam said, her tone turning formal, preparing for the encounter ahead. She looked up at the clear ceiling of the nav-com compartment, focused her thoughts and sent the diagnostic command.

"They're visible!" Fila said and swung the Q-Ship toward the targets. "I'll bet they're confused and that may give us extra time." Major Fila arranged the firing priorities with the ship's central computer and aimed the ship at the empty space between the three targets.

"Shields are Full, Cloaking and Sensor blocking on," Lieutenant Tam said as she verified the target positions and range. "Ten millipars to intercept."

⋏

When the escort fighters disappeared in separate, brilliant flashes, the patrol cruiser *Brigstoan* hailed the freighter and demanded it prepare for boarding or be disabled. When it did not respond, the *Brigstoan* fired a cannon volley across its bow and an irate response came from the freighter's communications officer. The Q-ship with a bright, diagonal red stripe across its fore body took up a position on the opposite side from the *Brigstoan* and both dropped their visual cloaking in a statement of superior strength. One more series of demands from the *Brigstoan* and the freighter reduced power and began boarding preparations.

Within a par, the *Brigstoan's* fifty aerial marines had secured the freighter. When the 'empty' ore containers were cracked and four envirocubes confirmed with between fifty and sixty captives in each, the freighter crew was interned aboard the *Brigstoan* and a pilot crew boarded to bring the freighter back to the Peace Force base in the Tunst System.

Thursday, December 22

Greg was quietly visiting with Coleen in the casual portion of the living room where she had taken a place on the loveseat near the fireplace and Greg was in his favorite overstuffed chair facing her. They were filling time before breakfast, again discussing some of the happenings since they had been separated when he was ten. Matti refilled his carafe of coffee and brought Coleen another cup of tea as she set a plate of sweet breads on the end table. "Will Mrs. Shara be joining you?" Matti asked when she stood up, ready to go back to the kitchen.

"In a little bit, Matti. She's just a little slow getting around this morning," Greg said absently.

Coleen glanced at Matti's curious expression, but did not say anything.

"Yes, Mr. Greg," Matti said. "Will she be having breakfast?"

"I suspect so," Greg said, "but we'll see."

Matti was almost to the kitchen when she turned and hurried to the back door. After a moment of quiet greetings, she led Kiile in through the dining room.

"Thank you, Matti," Greg said as he got up and greeted Kiile. Matti turned and went back to the kitchen.

"Colonel?" Kiile asked. "Can I take a moment of your time? Admiral Baker has sent a message."

Greg nodded and excused himself from Coleen for a moment and then led Kiile into the formal portion of the living room. He gestured to two chairs set close together at the front of the room.

"What's Baker have to say?" Greg asked as they sat down.

"He wants the 'parts' you offered," Kiile said with a broad smile.

"Very good," Greg smiled in return. "They will make both of our lives easier. When?"

"Next week sometime," Kiile said, sounding a little sheepish. "You said you were expecting a couple more Q-Ships, so I'll get billeting set up for them before we tackle the station. Are they paired crews or individuals?"

"Leeana was going to check, but she hasn't said what she's found out," Greg admitted.

"Well, that isn't a big concern," Kiile said continuing. "I'm thinking I will do an assessment flight up on Monday and maybe start lifting equipment on Tuesday. We'll have to work cloaked to keep the station's crew from seeing the obvious activity, but I think we can handle it."

"That should work," Greg admitted. "Let Baker know and do what you need to do. Are you going to be supervising the work?"

"The assessment, yes," Kiile said, "but I have some Techs that can handle the daily stuff."

"All right," Greg said and looked up as Shara came down the hall. "Anything else?"

Kiile smiled, seeing Greg's change in attention. "No sir. I think that's all for now."

"Are you free for Christmas dinner Sunday?" Greg asked, still watching Shara. "I know Shara will ask."

"Certainly, Colonel," Kiile said.

Greg realized Kiile wanted to ask something, but hesitated. "Yes, Kiile," he said with a smile. "Cheral will be here." Then he got up and met Shara in the dining room.

▲ ▲ ▲ ▲ ▲

"Abe," the voice said when Abe answered his phone console, "Don Nikle here. What's the word on our surveillance efforts?"

"Morning, Don," Abe said as he finished filling his coffee cup. "I'm still having some troubles."

"Now what?" Don's voice asked.

"I keep losing transmitters. I got one on the marshal's jeep yesterday morning," Abe said, "but he went to the Davis girls' house and parked it. It hasn't moved since then."

"Voice taps?"

"Nothing. Nothing from any of them," Abe said, his tone a little disgusted. "I'll double check again tonight to be sure they are still installed."

"I understand he's still asking questions," Don said.

"Not like he was," Abe said, "At least not from what I've been able to gather."

"I suspect the Davis girl has given him enough background to satisfy him then," Don surmised.

"Maybe, but she doesn't know anything more than the general public knows."

"Probably not," Don admitted, "but I understand she has his undivided attention."

"Yes," Abe agreed, "she does seem to."

"Find out what she really knows and what she's told him."

Friday, December 23

"I came by your place this afternoon," Wally was saying when he pulled into Carole's driveway. He had been waiting at midnight to drive her home, as had become their routine when she got off work. "Thom and Ted gave me a bit of news and I needed to look at your jeep."

"Why?" Carole asked, surprised.

"I'll show you," Wally replied, his tone somber, "if I can come in for a bit."

She smiled at him, "You know you don't have to ask if you can stay." The seriousness in his voice caught her attention. "Is there something wrong?"

He did not answer as he followed her in through the garage and waited for the door to close. Then when they were inside, he took her coat, hung it on the usual peg behind the front door and hung his beside it. When he turned to her, she was watching him, waiting.

"Maybe," he said cryptically and pulled two palm sized devices from his jacket pocket. "These," he continued when she looked at them, "are tracking and surveillance devices."

"Surveillance?" she asked and looked up at him.

He led her over to the living room couch and they sat down.

"Ted and Thom told me today," he began, "while you were talking with Mandy, they found similar devices planted under their patrol cars last Sunday and two of the voice transmitters planted at the office. When they removed them, another set showed up."

"What's that mean, Wally?" she asked as she settled close to him with her arm on the back of the couch and her hand on his shoulder.

"It means that the Family, probably the remaining Elders, want to know what the Deputies and I talk about," Wally explained, "and where we are at any given time. It's also possible they want to know what you've said to me."

She waited, mulling his words over.

"When they told me what they found," he said, "I got to thinking that they would want to put them on my patrol car and jeep, but I had the jeep with me and the patrol car in the garage."

"Okay. And?"

"Well, I figured they might have seen your jeep at my place Tuesday night thinking it was mine," he said and paused to hold her eyes. "So I came by here and found these when I checked your jeep."

She giggled. "They've been watching a jeep that hasn't gone anywhere in three days."

"Yeah," he agreed, "but that concerned me because they would know something was wrong with their plants. They have to know the deputies have been finding and removing them, and that means they'll try something else. At least, the guys have the remote checking their cars multiple times a day, and I added yours to its list. The remote will check yours when it scans ours."

"Well, you could give them what they want," Carole said with a wicked smile.

"You know, you're right," Wally said, catching her devious thought. "I'll take care of that when I leave."

"By the way," she said, changing the subject, "you are remembering you said you'd come for dinner tomorrow at Mom and Dad's, aren't you? And you're bringing the deputies and Dan's family on Sunday?"

"How could I forget," he smiled, put his arm around her and pulled her closer. "Two of your mom's wonderful dinners in one weekend. What time?"

"How early can you come?" she asked and laid her head on his shoulder. "Saturday dinner's probably about three and Sunday will be earlier, maybe one thirty or two. How about, maybe noon tomorrow?"

"I'll talk with the deputies, but I should be able to do noon tomorrow or a little after."

"Good," she said and kissed him.

▲ ▲ ▲ ▲ ▲

Ben leaned over Abe's shoulder as he added a new line of code on the computer screen.

"Will that do it?" Ben asked as Abe finished and hit Enter.

"I hope so," Abe admitted with a sigh, "I set up a directional receiver at your place and with the one here, we should be able to plot the position of a beacon on the display,"

"If they start transmitting," Ben said flatly. "I've put out, what, three on each of their cars and once on the marshal's jeep?"

"That's what you tell me," Abe said and compiled the new code.

"And I put a voice transmitter on two windows of that Carole Davis' house," Ben added, leaning a little farther over Abe's shoulder.

"That's good. Don wants to know what she's been telling the marshal."

When the compiling process finished, Abe cleared the screen and clicked the program icon. "Let's see what we have this time."

The program executed and a map of the town displayed over a large section of the monitor. Abe clicked a menu pull-down and selected one of the four beacon IDs he had loaded.

"Aah, that looks good," he said as a blue dot appeared on the screen. "Looks like it's parked in front of the marshal's office."

"It's working!" Ben shouted.

"Easy, Ben," Abe said and selected three more beacon IDs from the menu of ten. "Now that's a lot better," he said as another dot appeared in another color.

"Which one's the marshal's dot?" Ben asked as he leaned

closer to the screen.

"He's the red one," Abe said, pointing to the dot as it moved down Main and turned in front of the square marked as Hap's Place. Abe quickly selected the rest of the IDs, knowing some weren't broadcasting a signal. He was pleased when the other two dots appeared.

"How far can you track them?" Ben persisted with his questions.

"About a mile and a half," Abe frowned. "This stupid valley won't let a signal get very far before it swallows it up."

"Well at least we can follow them around town," Ben said.

That'll be a big help," Abe admitted and turned to the phone console. "Maybe this will get Don off our backs for a little while."

C.3482.376

Chairman Sorgat looked at the identification screen when the interoffice communications console buzzed. He knew the message would not be a good one.

"Greetings Director Kraast," he said and paused the scrolling on the screen floating above his desk. "Guessing by the time, I suspect something new has happened."

"Unfortunately, yes, Chairman Sorgat," the intelligence director's voice admitted.

The chairman waited.

"Sir," Director Kraast continued, "we have just received a message fragment sent from a contract freighter that departed the Trader's secreted facility on Betolle enroute to a stop in the Daneets System for an additional cargo pickup."

Again the chairman waited and stared at the communications video screen.

Director Kraast wet his lips and then continued. "They reported they had been intercepted by a Peace Force patrol cruiser with a heavy fighter escort. They were boarded and the message ended suddenly when the Peace Force Marines seized the bridge. The crew and cargo are feared to be captured by the Peace Force."

The chairman's shoulders sagged and his voice turned dour. "When?"

"C.3482.374," the director said. "Three standard turns past, at 1740 galactic standard time."

"Two turns after the loss of the supply freighter in terran space," the Chairman said absently. "It does make it look like Director Ahaar did arouse the interest of the Peace Force after all." He paused and then continued, "Did you contact the second launch facility?"

"Yes, sir," Director Kraast's voice said, sounding a little more pleased. "They have transportation operational and can manage supplies. Funds must be transferred if they are to do without space side supplies."

"Yes, yes," the chairman said gruffly. "And can they do any investigation at the data complex or around Point Obscure?"

"They said they can," Director Kraast confirmed. "They will report what they find, but they cautioned that it will take a little time. They fear the heavy surveillance that has stopped all previous attempts to collect information. They will proceed slowly."

"Yes," the chairman agreed. "Make the necessary transfers and get them started. We are fighting blind without information."

"At once, Chairman," the director said and the chairman disconnected the console with a gruff slap of his hand.

With the house quiet and closed up for the night, Shara and Greg settled into bed. The two remotes watched over the ranch perimeter, both roads approaching the ranch and made a periodic swing around town, listening for anything unusual in the fabric of the night.

Shara snuggled between the fleece sheets with the quilt bed cover over them. She held Greg tight, happy for the way things were for the moment.

"You were very quiet tonight, Bren," Greg said as he tilted her head back and kissed her.

"Just a lot to think about," she answered, avoiding the details.

"Well," he said softly, "I think the girls have done an incredible job of preparing for the holidays. I don't think they have let our plans stress them a bit."

"Matti is very good at arranging and getting things done. She's been a real blessing for me," she admitted. "And I'm glad you are getting some time to get to know your mother."

"I'm glad too," he admitted. "There's so much we've missed."

"In a way I can relate to that," she said and tightened her arms around him. "In my case, my mother was here all the time and we still missed having a relationship."

"I know," he admitted, "and I've been on my own for so long, without a family until you and I made one, that it's a little difficult for me..."

"To open up to someone?" she asked.

"Yes, but it isn't like opening up to you and sharing everything I do or think with you," he said, gently caressing her back. "With you, sharing everything is so natural, so normal. You're so much a part of me. But with her and Brendan, I still feel very guarded, cautious."

"You have to be, love," Shara said almost in a whisper. "But I have to admit, I was surprised with how open you were with me after we met."

"I've known you longer," he smiled, "Even if it was one sided for many years." Again, he tilted her head back and kissed her.

'COLONEL, LIEUTENANT. MAY I INTERRUPT?' STSX

said in their minds.

'*Yes. What is it?*' Greg answered.

'*DIRECTOR AGL36Q HAS SENT A MESSAGE. THE DIRECTOR APOLOGIZES FOR INITIATING AN ENGAGEMENT IN YOUR COMMAND WITHOUT ADVISING YOU FIRST. HE DISPATCHED A PEACE FORCE PATROL CRUISER AND A Q-SHIP TO INTERCEPT AND BOARD A TRADER'S UNION FREIGHTER OUT OF BETOLLE. THREE KYDDELLAN ESCORT FIGHTERS DESTROYED. OVER TWO HUNDRED CAPTIVES FOUND AND RELEASED. CREW INCARCERATED. FREIGHTER COMMANDEERED AND CONFISCATED. DIRECTOR HAS ISSUED STANDING ORDERS TO INVESTIGATE ALL SUSPICIOUS FREIGHTER ACTIVITIES, ESPECIALLY FREIGHTERS WITH HEAVY KYDDELLAN FIGHTER ESCORTS. ALL TERRAN CAMPAIGN WATCHERS NOW CARRY ABLE SQUADRON'S RED STRIPE. EOM.*'

'*Thanks, STSX,*' Greg said. '*Reply message received. Apology accepted.*'

"So, it's started?" Shara asked softly. "Does this mean the director is taking your suspicions seriously?"

"Yes, Bren," Greg sighed, rolled onto his back and pulled her with him. "It also seems the director is honoring his promise to brand all of the involved Q-Ships with Apache Squadron's colors, your headband. I think the director is listening to everything you and I tell him."

She made herself comfortable and looked down at him in the dim light. "I guess we better be careful and not tell him everything we think about." She lowered her head and kissed him and let the moments drift by without counting.

Eighty-Six
Saturday, December 24

In his bath robe and carrying a large mug of coffee, Abe slowly walked from his kitchen into his den and dropped into the chair in front of the tracking screen. He forced his eyes to stay open and sipped at the hot brew, hoping the sugar he added would kick in and help wake him up.

Absently glancing over the quiet screen, not expecting the dots to be moving much at this hour on a Saturday morning, he tapped a code into the adjacent keyboard and waited for the voice recordings to begin a replay. He waited.

When a moment had passed with no sound, he began to check his cabling, and once satisfied everything was still connected, he scrolled the files, hoping that in his sleepy state he had simply tagged the wrong files for replay. He search again and again found the file for the previous night, but he nearly spilled his coffee when he realized the file size was zero, empty! No data!

"What! Where are you?" he asked himself in disbelief.

He scrolled the file list a second time and when the results were the same, he keyed for a signal interrogation routine. After a minute of activity, the program displayed a 'No Signal' icon.

Abe sorted through the programs and tried alternate interrogation routines, but the answer was the same; the transmitters were not sending any data of any kind.

Muttering something about Ben's inability to do the simplest tasks, he toggled the phone console for Ben's number. "Ben," he asked in a dry voice, when the connection made and Ben answered. "Are you sure you put those transmitters on the windows?"

181

"Oh, hello Abe," Ben's groggy voice came back. "Yup, just like you told me to."

"Did you check to be sure they were turned on?"

"Sure," he answered. "The little blue light blinked ten times and then went out, like it is supposed to. Why?"

"They have not transmitted anything," Abe said, trying to hold his temper and tongue.

"How can that be, Abe?" Ben asked. "Like I told you, I put one on the living room window and one on the bedroom window, on the glass."

Abe shook his head and inhaled slowly. "I don't know why they are not working, but watch her house today and when you're certain no one is there, I want you to check and be sure they are turned on."

"Abe," Ben said, concern coloring his voice. "Don says not to be seen. Work at night only."

"Yeah, okay," Abe conceded. "Tonight, after dark, when no one can see you, I want you to check then and make sure they are working."

▲ ▲ ▲ ▲ ▲

Little Carrie Anne had tolerated the after dinner small talk as long as she could and she began to squirm in her booster chair, playing with her dishes and dropping her spoon, giggling every time Marty picked it up for her. Finally, Marty let her get down and took her into the spacious living room to let the conversations continue around the dinner table without further distractions.

Wally leaned back and looked around the large dining room and into the high, vaulted living room graced with the large Christmas tree and decorations, momentarily engrossed in the rustic splendor of Carole's folk's timber main house. He enjoyed his talks with Carole's brother in-law, Jim, and smiled to himself at Carole's obvious pleasure when he and his family were able to come back to Riggin for a visit. He remembered she told him they had been back more often this fall than in all of the past four years.

When Jim got up and went to rescue Marty from the unrelenting demands of his daughter, Wally tried to help Rusty with clearing the table. But as she did on his previous visits, Rusty turned Wally to the living room and pressed her daughters into the task. Reluctantly, Wally took a seat at one end of the long couch and watched Jim roll on the floor, wrestling with his almost three year old.

"Well, how was your trip?" Marty asked Wally as he sat down in his favorite overstuffed chair. He turned to have a comfortable view of both the fireplace and the front window with its vista beyond.

"It was good," he admitted, "filled with mostly formalities, paperwork and meetings."

"George Hattle tells me," Marty continued, "that your promotion will let you stay here if you want."

Jim stopped and cradled Carrie Anne in his arms as he looked up to see Wally's reaction.

"Yes," Wally said slowly. "I talked to the director of Law Enforcement and he confirms that the marshal's position is permanent if I want it to be. No elections necessary, and I can keep a team of deputies as long as I feel I need them, also permanent if they want it to be. And as you probably know, there's still a lot going on that we need to take care of. A lot of folks are still very uncomfortable and unsure of the future. Who's on which side and who's winning."

Marty studied the view of the valley through the large front window as it stretched out below the ranch and Jim slowly returned his attention to his giggling daughter.

"Have you decided what you want to do?" Marty asked without looking away from the window.

Wally hesitated and glanced at Marty's profile before he answered. "I have, but there's a small detail I have to work out first."

Marty looked at him, but kept his expression blank.

Wally was about to add that it was a personal issue when Carole and Shelly came into the room. Rusty folded a damp dishtowel over the back of a dining room chair and followed the girls as Carole took her place beside Wally.

Their conversation was casual and he enjoyed the minutes until he finally pushed himself up off the couch and thanked Rusty for the wonderful dinner, explaining that he had to get ready for the evening rounds.

"Are you still coming for Christmas dinner tomorrow?" Rusty asked as she gave him a hug.

"Yes," he said with a smile. "How could I possibly turn down an invitation to another of your wonderful meals, and the opportunity to spend another special day with you and your family? Thank you very much."

He turned and thanked Marty and said his goodbyes to Jim and Shelly with a special pat on Carrie's head. Carole was waiting at the front door, handed him his jacket and slipped hers on as she followed him out.

▲

"Wish you didn't have to go so soon," she said as he stopped and absently caressed the hood of his new jeep with the State Marshal's star extending to its edges.

He turned, slipped his arms around her shoulders and pulled her close. "Me either, but..."

She tilted her head back and looked up at him.

He smiled. "I was wondering if you would consider living your life with me. Going wherever life takes us, together?"

"Wally?" Her smile faded slightly. "What are you asking? Really?"

His smile widened. "I want to marry you, Carole. I'm asking if you would share my life, be my wife, wherever our life would take us."

She pulled back from him, her smile faded, her body shook and her eyes watered. "Oh Wally. Don't do this to me. I can't just go 'wherever.' My life is here. I..."

Wally dropped his shoulders and released her. He felt like she'd slugged him in the gut. "I see." He looked at her for a long moment. "I can't see my life continuing the way it was. Our time together has been... and I thought you... I guess I misunderstood," he sighed and opened his door. "I'm sorry, Carole."

"Wally, please. There are things you don't understand," she said softly as her eyes filled. "Please believe me. I want—"

"It's okay, Carole," he said, his legs going weak as he fell into the seat and closed the door. "I do understand. I just thought we..." He shook his head involuntarily, "Maybe this is for the best."

He started the jeep, slowly backed out of the parking space.

▲

Carole's eyes filled with tears as she watched Wally back away from her, and suddenly her temper flared. She darted into the drive, stopped and turned in front of his jeep.

"Wally Lima! Stop!" she shouted and grabbed the top of the brush guard as he slammed on the brakes. She stared at him, getting angrier by the second.

"You DON'T understand!" she shouted. She jerked the passenger door open and jumped in. "And you're going to listen to me! Right now!"

He stared at her but did not let the jeep move as she took a deep breath and forced her temper down.

"Park the jeep, Wally," she finally said in as near a normal voice as she could manage. "There are things you have to know."

Slowly Wally put the jeep back into the parking spot and shut it down. "Okay. I'm listening," he said impassively and turned to face her.

She inhaled again and held his eyes. "There is a set of conditions that my grandparents laid down before they died and I have to abide by them."

His look turned to puzzlement.

185

"My grandparents bought and set aside a parcel of land," she said slowly. "A rather large parcel of land. And they originally left it to my brother, my sister and me as long as we meet the conditions they set forth."

"Okay," Wally said softly. "I think that's nice that they did that for you, but—"

"Wally," she interrupted. "I'm the only one of us kids that hasn't broken the conditions. And I'm not going to lose that parcel and let it go for sale or to auction."

"I wouldn't ask you to," he said, still puzzled.

"You asked me to go with you 'wherever' life would take us," she said and looked out through the windshield. "But I can't. If I leave the valley and live anywhere else before I've been married for ten years, or reach forty, I'll lose it all." She slowly turned to look at him. "My brother Todd left the valley to live somewhere else. He's been gone for over four years now, so he forfeited his claim to the land or any part of it. And Shelly, when she married Jim and they moved away, and are now living in Lynchburg, she forfeited her claim as well. I'm the last heir and I won't leave the valley. It's what I've wanted all my life. The only thing I've wanted," she wiped her eyes on her coat sleeve, "until I met you. Please, don't make me choose."

"Carole," Wally said softly, taking her hand from her lap. "I wasn't asking you to leave the valley. But a life together will lead us to places we haven't been before, even while living here. Maybe I stated it wrong, but a life together will be different."

Carole stared at him for a long moment, slowly feeling the sincerity in his words.

"I told you after we met that I like it here," he said. "And you said you've always wanted to be a rancher. Remember?"

"Are you sure you want to be tied down here?" Carole asked, uncertainty still tugging at her heart. "If your job takes you somewhere else, I'll have to stay here."

"Even while I was hopelessly falling for you," he explained, "I was afraid the day would come that I would have to leave you. I couldn't ask you to marry me unless I could offer you support and a stable home here, for us and maybe a family when you're ready. As a special state deputy, jumping from one assignment to another, I couldn't offer you any of that."

"I worried about that too," she said and squeezed his hand.

"While I was over at the capital, I confirmed my new position is permanent if I choose it to be," he smiled, "as permanent as anything can be. If we're together, I want to stay here. If we're not, then I probably won't."

She smiled, wrapped her arm around his neck and pulled him closer, kissing him firmly. "You'd really do that for me? Stay here and put up with all of this?"

"Only if the bargain means I get to keep you," he said with a smile.

She kissed him again and then asked, "What was that question you asked me?"

"You mean the one about whether you'd marry me?"

"Yeah," she said and kissed him again. "That's the one."

And?"

"Yeah, I think I will."

"You're sure?" He waited until she nodded, getting another kiss for his wait. "Good," he said and reached into his coat pocket. "Then I should give you one of your Christmas presents early." He handed her the small box as she relaxed and straightened up.

She unwrapped and opened the box, but could only stare at the beautifully crafted pair of rings.

"They're really beautiful, Wally," she said as he took the engagement ring from the box.

He slipped the ring on her finger, pleased that he had sized it correctly.

She studied the sculptured gold swirls, with small imbedded diamonds wrapping partway around and protecting the oval, master diamond. "I can even wear riding or work gloves without hurting it."

"I remembered you talking about Shar's ring," he said, "and how the low setting took care of that."

Then she looked up at him, "How can a marshal pay for something like this, even if he's a special state marshal?"

"Now, now," he said and kissed her again. "Let's not start arguing over money so soon." Then he took her hand, "I get paid reasonably well and I haven't spent money on anything for the last ten years, as you can see from my house. So I've just saved up for things I might need someday. But the sale of my old jeep and the bonus and allowance I got with my promotion, more than covered the expenses in this case."

"Thanks for letting me explain, Wally," she said and looked at her ring again.

"And thanks for stopping me and making me listen," he said. Smiling, he could not resist and kissed her again. "But just for my curiosity, why is the land your grandparents set aside so important to you, besides the obvious that you want to be a rancher?"

"Well," she started slowly, "as you've pointed out, I did tell you that I've always wanted to be a horse rancher and ranchers need land. For starters, the parcel in question is almost sixty-five thousand acres. Together with mom and dad's ranch, it's more than half the size of Shar's ranch and nearly one tenth the size of the Rockin' H. It's the third largest parcel in the northern valley."

"Wow," Wally whispered. "I'd no idea..."

She studied his expression and slowly smiled. "For half my life, I've had to fend off the boys here in the valley. They only saw me as a way to get their hands on that land. I kept waiting, hoping to meet someone I liked that didn't have land on the brain, and then I met you. When I started liking you, I was afraid that you'd find out and turn out to be another one of them."

"Well, I'm not," he said softly, "but it'll be nice to help you develop it into whatever you're planning to do with it. It's yours, not mine. You can even put that in a prenup if you want."

"Thank you, Wally," she said and pulled him close again.

"Now, Miss Davis," he said formally, "I have to make the evening rounds with Ted. Will I see you later or do I have to wait until tomorrow?"

"Later," she said. "I'll be in around ten or so and I'll stop by your place."

⬥

"Well that took a while," Rusty said as Carole came back into the house. "Did I hear you yelling at him?"

"Yeah," she said with a smile and slowly flopped down on the couch beside Shelly. "We had a few things to talk out."

"Talk out?" Shelly asked. "Was there a misunderstanding?"

"Not once I explained it," she said and looked sideways at Shelly with a slowly growing smile. Then she held her hand up, "He asked."

Shelly's eyes went wide and Rusty was up and beside her in a second.

"Obviously you said 'yes,'" Shelly said, turning Carole's hand one way and then the other.

Rusty looked the ring over, smiled hugely and caught Carole's eye. "So you explained it?" she repeated Carole's words as a question. "You told him?"

"Yes," Carole said, seeing the concern flash behind her mother's eyes. "He didn't know. Seeing his reaction, I am completely sure he didn't know. He even said I could put it in a prenup if I wanted to."

"Good for you, girl. Now, you better go tell your father your good news," Rusty said, smiling as she got up. "He's out by the barn with Jim, getting more wood for the fireplace."

Sunday, December 25

Christmas Day

A light snow had started falling about daybreak and filled

the valley with dense fog. The fire in the fireplace was warm and the huge tree stood dominant in the vaulted timber living room of the main house. Greg and Shara came out of the bedroom wing and checked the preparations for the morning. With Greg's help, Shara confirmed there were appropriate presents under the tree and all of the food stuffs that Annie and the girls needed for the main meal were neatly stored in the pantry and cold rooms off the kitchen. Annie had stirred Matti and Cara early, getting preparations started and the meats slowly roasting in the ovens.

Annie greeted them as she set a platter of her sweet breads and cakes on the table beside the bowls of fruits. Matti and Cara placed carafes of juice, coffee and tea between it and a small pyramid of cups and glasses. With the large dinner planned for the midafternoon meal, breakfast was simply morning snacks and drinks.

Shara sat in her customary place on Greg's lap, nibbled on a cinnamon flavored sweet roll and sipped her coffee. Greg held her gently against him as he sipped from his own cup, accepted an occasional, proffered bite of Shara's roll and waited for everyone else to get up and join them.

"I remember," Shara was saying softly, "so many Christmases in this room. Each year the tree was placed a little different, but most of the time it was in that same corner so people coming to visit would see the lights as they came up the drive." She looked at him and smiled. "And now, after all that has happened, I'm so very glad to add our first Christmas together, here in the same room."

"Well, Bren," he replied happily, "I'm glad to finally be a part of your memories," he clinked his cup against hers, "and hope to make many more happy ones for you in the future."

When Coleen and Brendan came out, Shara and Greg got up, greeted them and gestured to the table.

"Breakfast is as light or as heavy as you'd like to make it," Shara said, "Lunch will more than fill any emptiness left. How'd you two sleep? Too warm? Cold?"

"Just fine," Coleen said and poured herself a cup of tea. "Temperature was just right and the room was as comfortable as we remembered it."

Brendan filled a small plate and found a chair near the living room end of the table and sat down. After a long sip of coffee, he blinked his eyes and smiled. "Aah. I think I'll live."

Coleen chuckled at him, "He's not much good until he has his first cup of coffee."

"Morning," Jill greeted, seeming to be more awake and alert than her usual early morning self as she entered the dining room. But she sniffed the air, headed for the table and found the stack of coffee cups.

"I see Brendan isn't the only one," Coleen greeted as Jill poured from a carafe.

The back door opened and Nick entered, leading Leeana and Major Kooich in. Everyone made their greetings and Shara called the house girls and Hank and the hands in to join them in the living room. When they had found chairs or floor space to settle on, Shara passed out the gifts from under the tree, making certain that each person got something personal from her and Greg. In addition, Matti and the girls and Hank and the hands each got a card with a generous Christmas bonus. Major Kooich and Leeana received light weight, western themed quilts for their use on KKLC14, or wherever else they might be, and Coleen and Brendan received framed photo-portraits, one of the four of them on horseback, taken on their previous and first visit to the ranch, another of Greg and Shara together and Greg gave Coleen a framed picture of just the two of them.

Shara admired the warm yellow full body robe Greg gave her, like Cheral's robe she had used while recovering on STSX, with elastic cuffs at the wrists and ankles. Greg was pleased with the curled brim western hat that Shara gave him, and wore it until they settled around the table for breads and beverages.

"Major," Shara asked after the general conversations had gone their courses, "Will you and Leeana be able to make dinner today?"

"I believe we will," he said and glanced at Leeana. "The Q-Ships and the cadets have arranged their schedules for station escort duties and the patrol of the valley. They worked it so we don't have our turn until later in the afternoon." Then seeing a question in Shara's eyes, he added, "Cheral volunteered for a mid to late morning time so she could be here as well," he looked at the time. "Actually, Cheral and Ani Tigs should already be up."

Shara smiled and relaxed a little. "That'll be nice. Since Cheral wasn't here, I suspected she was on duty."

"So, Shar?" Jill asked, "Who's going to be here today? Your dinner guests?"

"Not that many, Jill," Shara said and refilled her coffee. "The six of us here, since you said you and Nick were going over to your folk's place, Kiile and Cheral and Paul, Hank and the three hands, the three house girls, the other two cadets, and Rose and Doug. Twenty, I think." She ticked the list off on her fingers. "Yes, that's it. Jim, Shelly and Carrie Anne are over at Shelly's folk's place and I believe Gary and Bill are joining them there. Rusty invited the new deputies and Deputy Lupis' wife and daughter also." She smiled and looked around the table, "And I heard it's a special Christmas for the Davis's as well."

"Special?" Jill asked and Coleen looked at her in question.

"Yup," Shara smiled and glanced at Greg's nod. "Remote Five told us yesterday that Wally asked Carole to marry him."

Jill's expression went quickly from surprise to concern. "Oh my. Does that mean he knows about the conditions?"

"He didn't," Shara admitted. "He almost left when she was reluctant to answer him, but she made him listen and she explained the details. In the end, he was okay with it and she said 'yes.'"

"We don't understand," Coleen said and Brendan, Major Kooich and Leeana all admitted they were also in the dark.

Jill and Shara explained Carole's grandparent's stipulations.

"Must be something for her to want it above all else,"

Coleen said softly.

"Maybe not above everything else, Coleen," Shara explained, "but around here, for someone with ranching in their blood and who wants to be a rancher, the land is essential. Since Uncle Paul claimed all he could when he settled in the north valley, there isn't a lot of it available for other ranches. He was a little selfish. And the parcel Carole will 'earn' is significant, half again the size of Nick's Dad's place, south east of here and more than half the size of ours."

The discussion of land and ranching dominated the conversation for most of the remaining morning. Coleen and Brendan were eager to learn all they could about Shara's way of life and how Greg and Shara saw it affecting their life together. Major Kooich and Leeana had seen and lived with the interaction between Greg and Shara and the way they blended their separate interests, but to hear the background and the family histories was a greatly appreciated view of the two most important and interesting people in their lives.

Shara got up and took a carafe to the kitchen to refill it, but as she pushed the door open, she froze and the words spilled out, "Greg! Cheral's in trouble!"

⚔ ⚔ ⚔ ⚔ ⚔

"Q-LTVC21, Apache Patrol Two and Three joining up from behind," Cheral said into her helmet mike as they approached the S.S. QuickSilver and its escort in trail.

"Good morning, Patrol Two and Three," Lieutenant Debira's voice replied. "Good to have you up. The morning has been quiet. Our periodic broadcasts have not shown any unexpected activity."

"Apache Patrol Three, move to the right side about a mile out and a mile in trail," Cheral said, then back to LTVC21, "We've got the baton. You might as well go and enjoy the day."

"Thanks Apache Patrol Two," Lieutenant Debira said. "We'll

see you two after your turn. First round is on me."

"Thanks, Lieutenant. We'll see you down stairs after a bit," Cheral agreed and watched LTVC21's target slide out of formation and begin their descent. "Apache Patrol Three, Systems check."

"All essential systems are green. Cloaking and Sensor Blocking are on and Shields are Full." Cheral followed Ani's words with the checks in her own cockpit. "Weapons are peaked."

"Very good," Cheral said when the list was completed.

After falling with the space station for nearly three quarters of an hour, enjoying the magnificent view of the planet below the infinite star field around them and routinely scanning for visitors, Ani broke the silence.

"Captain?" Ani asked. "Who's broadcasting the cloaking transmitter codes? We were told that they had to be sent empathically. I'm not good enough yet to do that. Are you?"

"Today it's STSX1," Cheral replied. "Squad Leader Kiile told me that his surveillance team and STSX1 alternate days when STSX1 is planet side. Otherwise, it's Kiile's group or one of the other Q-Ship crews."

"Thank you, Captain," Ani said formally. "I was just wondering."

"I also heard that next week," Cheral continued, "they are going to install Shields and two cannon turrets on the space station. Plus there is talk of giving them a com-link so whoever is on escort duty can communicate with them if the need arises."

"I bet the colonel's visit raised a lot of questions," Ani said absently.

"Yes it did," Cheral admitted. "But the admiral finally agreed to letting us install the changes. Uh oh."

"What do you have, ma'am?" Ani asked, quickly scanning her consoles. "Ship problem?"

"No. A target, down low," she answered, startled as she

realized she felt its presence and nothing was showing on the scanner. Then she switched to her normal communications channels. "Apache Base. Apache Patrol Two is tracking a low altitude target near the south end of the valley. Do you have an ID?"

A short moment passed. "Apache Patrol Two. Base has nothing painted. Codes do not illuminate any targets."

"Thanks," Cheral said and switched back to the inter-ship channel. "Ani, I'm going down to take a look. You stay with the station. You're its wingman, its protection while I'm gone. I'll see if Apache Four can come up and I'll be back up as soon as I can. Keep your com-links open and listen."

"Yes, Captain," Ani replied. "I'll be here, listening."

Cheral eased her fighter into a descent and maneuvered to approach the target from farther south, hoping to follow it as it wandered up the foggy valley.

"Apache Base, Apache Patrol Two," Cheral said, opening the link again. "Is Cadet Moss available in Apache Patrol Four?"

A moment went by. "Negative. He's still having troubles with ship Four. Tests this morning went badly."

"Is there anyone available for a short escort duty?" she asked.

"Everyone is working to an assigned slot," Apache Base replied, "Unless you have an emergency?"

"Negative, Base, no emergency," Cheral said. Ani would know she would just have to wait alone.

It took longer than Cheral wanted, but she finally worked her way down to the target's altitude and fell in behind it. The fog was thicker in the south valley, hindering all physical vision, but as she got closer, the details of her sensation got clearer and stronger. She felt an odd energy that seemed to pulse from one side of the target to the other side.

"STSX," she called softly into her helmet mike. "Can you analyze the sensation I am having?"

"YES. ONE MAN FIGHTER USING SEARCH PROBE

SWEEPS. THE TARGET IS LOOKING FOR SOMETHING," STSX answered.

"Can you hail the target and demand it land immediately?" she asked, uncertain of what she should do next. "Probably should alert Kiile that it's here."

STSX hailed the fighter, but instead of capitulating, the fighter quickly rotated and started a vertical climb.

"He's going to break for it," Cheral said and pulled her patrol fighter up to give chase.

She held onto the ship's presence and accelerated, closing quickly. Just out of the atmosphere, she felt three other sensations, very small and traveling back toward her. "Damn! Mines!"

In reflex, she fired all four cannons and jinked the patrol fighter sideways as the target disappeared in a brilliant ball of flames and smoke; the first mine hit her shields. The flash blinded her for a moment and the jolt spun the fighter into the path of the second mine and the explosion depleted the shield's energy banks. They collapsed just as the third mine sped past and detonated just behind her.

'Shhaaarrr!' her mind screamed in sudden pain. She yelled again and tried to shake the bright spots from her eyes. Then slowly, as if she was watching through someone else's eyes, the spots faded and the unbelievably battered image of her cockpit came into focus. She saw the wide expanse of the planet beyond it. Someone was talking to her, but she could not get her mind to listen to the words.

What happened? she wondered, her mind thick as syrup, unable to think clearly. *Canopy's shattered, the right half of the panels are unrecognizable.* She turned her head to look to her right, her neck painfully arguing against her movement, and she realized the right side of the cockpit was missing. She twisted, searing pain swept up her right side and across her back, stealing her breath away. Frozen in agony, she realized she was sitting in a gaping maw with nothing beside her but the vast expanse between her and the planet below. Then she saw the red fog drifting beside her and knew her pressure suit was punctured; they were both leaking. Reluctantly, knowing she did not want to know, she glanced at the suit's wrist indicators, confirming her race with fate.

'*Shar, I'm losing suit pressure. Down to point two of normal. Four, maybe five minutes max. The ship's severely damaged. Can't bring it down. I think...*' Her words slowed, slurred and stretched out as her vision slowly dimmed. '*...it's too late... to be an Emergency now.*'

'*You hold on, Cuz. We're almost there.*'

Shara and Greg's dangerous journey continues in
Paladin Shadows Series Book 8;
Operation Retribution Part 2, Taking the Fight Off World.

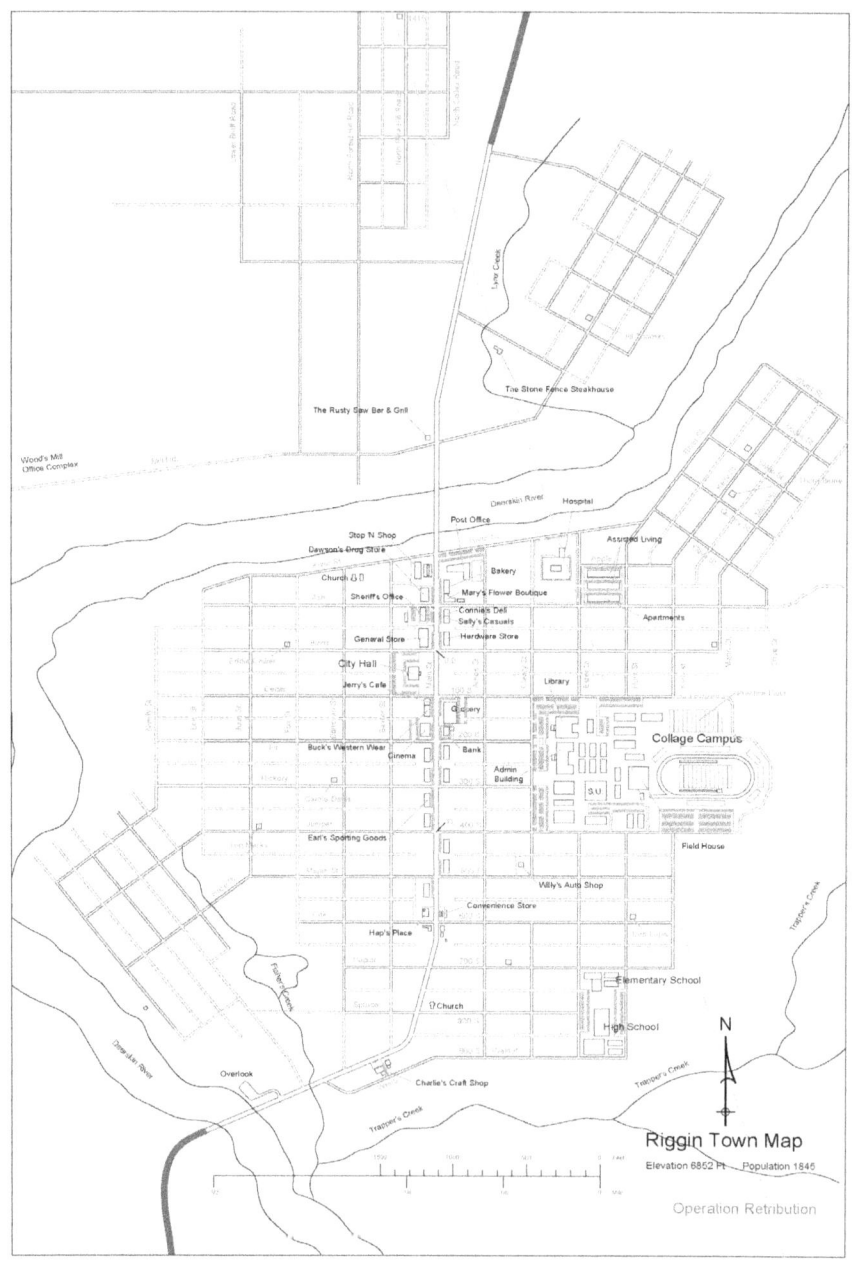

Riggs Valley Map

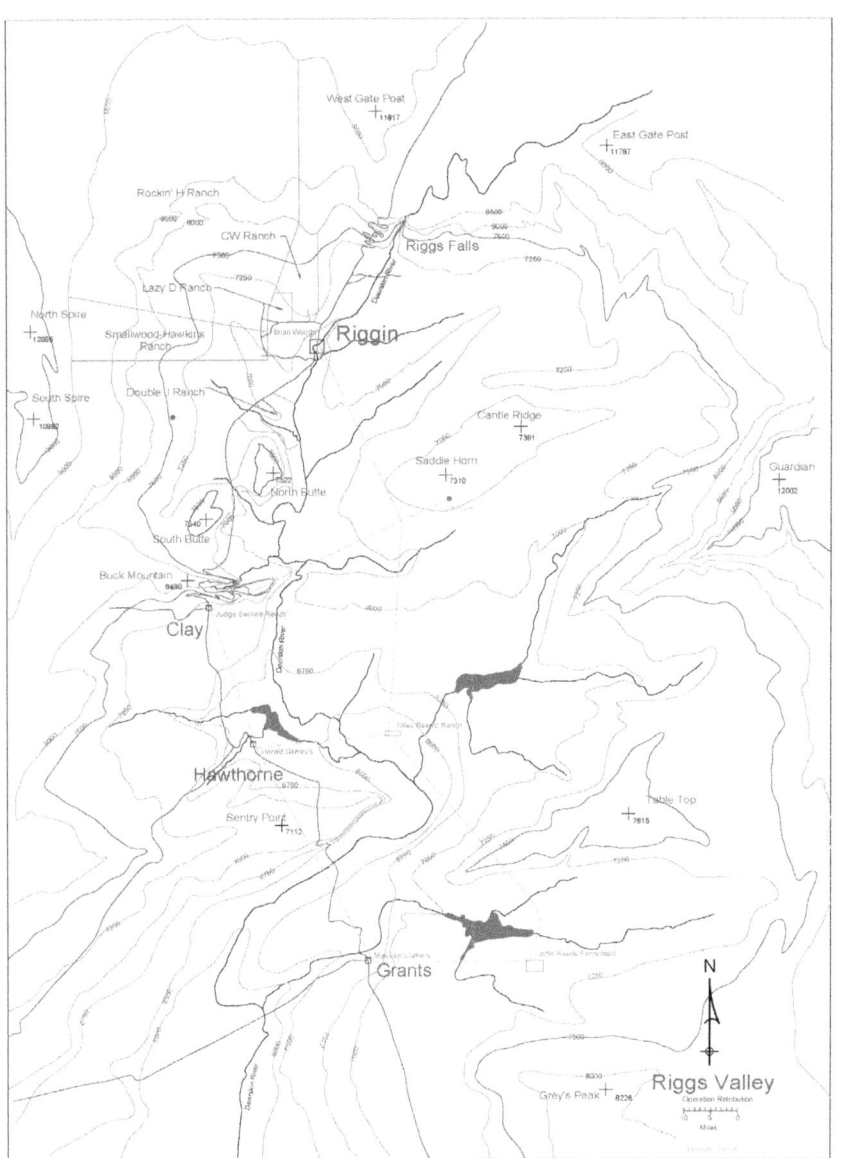

Glossary

Characters:

-A-

Ahaar — Key agent for the Trader's Union.

Arkir, Captain — Captain of the freighter, Dai Horizon.

-B-

Bernice Reeds; Judge — See Reeds, Bernice; Judge

Bren — Short version of Greg's nickname, 'BrenCara,' for Shara. Old Country meaning: "Special Raven Haired Friend."

-C-

Cadet Pilots — Cadet students training in the art of space combat.

Apache Patrol Two: Captain Cheral Haak

Apache Patrol Three: Cadet Ani Tigs

Apache Patrol Four: Cadet Wilm Moss

Apache Patrol Five: Cadet Loni Grenn (Reported Jan 11)

Apache Patrol Six: Cadet Gill Kast (Reported Jan 11)

Camerso — Gentleman's Gentleman to Prince Kiese.

Cara — Second house girl at the Smallwood-Hawkins Ranch.

Cassel, Brendan — Coleen Malone's second husband, mate. (IAL01-SS3)

Cassel, Coleen — Husband/mate to Brendan Cassel, second marriage. Previous marriage: Coleen Reese. Maiden name: Coleen

201

	Malone.
Chairman Sorgat	Principal Officer in the Trader's Union
Clark, Della	Daughter of Widow Clark and sister of Steve. College student in Riggin.
Coleen Malone	See Malone, Coleen
Coleen Reese	See Reese, Coleen
Colette Marsin	See Marsin, Colette
Collier, Eddie	Floral Arranger at Mary's Flower Boutique. 23 yrs old. Daughter of Daniel Collier. No siblings.
Collier, Daniel	Eddie's missing father.

-D-

Danley, Harold	Banker in Clay, one of Bernice's Elders.
Danny	Shara's black stallion.
Davis, Carole	Waitress at Hap's Place. Shelly's younger sister by one year. 23 yrs of age.
Davis, Marty	Married to Rusty Davis. Father of Shelly, Carole and Todd Davis.
Davis, Rusty	Married to Marty Davis. Mother of Shelly, Carole and Todd Davis.
Davis, Shelly	Raised in Riggin, wife of Lt. Jim Woods. Mother of Carrie Anne Woods. 24 yrs of age.
Davis, Todd	Older brother of Shelly and Carole Davis. Moved away from the valley before Shelly graduated from high school.
Deputies, Special	Thom Baine. See Baine, Thom.
	Dan Lupis. See Lupis, Dan.

Ted Marks. See Marks, Ted.

Dílis	Shara's black-faced roan. Greg's favorite and named by him. (Pronounced Jee + lus)
Director Korveel	Merchandise Director for the Trader's Union.
Director, Peace Force	Identification AGL36Q

-E-

Elders, The Family	Brian Woods (deceased)
	Harry Woods (deceased)
	Harold Danley (captured)
	Malcolm Clotter (captured)
	Charley Clotter (captured)
	Dave Barns
	Don Nikle

-G-

Geaardt, Stran	A Shadow. An undercover agent. A Major in the Galactic Peace Force. GPF ID: HQZL09-ES. Pronounced "Gee (as in Geese), + art."
Geaardt, Casi (Casey)	A Shadow. An undercover agent. Stran Geaardt's partner, wife. HQZL09-ES2 GPF ID. Pronounced 'Casey.'
Geaardt, Moira	Registered name of Coleen Malone
Greg Malone	See Malone, Greg
Grenn, Loni	Cadet Pilot of Apache Patrol Five, Class 1 Patrol Fighter.

-H-

Haak, Cheral	Captain in the Galactic Peace Force. Cadet in the Peace Force Flight Academy. Cadet Pilot of

	Apache Two, Class 2 Patrol Fighter. Granddaughter of Paal Haak. Previous Upper-Lieutenant Nav-Com on Q-STSX1.
Haak, Paal	Commander, Galactic Peace Force Academy, Retired. Grandfather to Cheral Haak
Hank	Forman at the Smallwood Ranch.
Hawkins, Andrew	Deceased brother of Paul and Nancy Hawkins. Married Katherine Reeds. Father of Clea Hawkins. Shara's Grandfather.
Hawkins, Nancy	Sister of Paul and Andrew Hawkins. Second wife of Dave Ashley, no children.
Hawkins, Paul	Brother of Andrew and Nancy Hawkins.
Hawkins, Clea	Unplanned daughter of Andrew Hawkins and Katherine Reeds. Married to Henry Smallwood. Mother of Shara, and surrogate to two daughters.

-J-

Jordan, Robert (Bob)	Owner of the Jordan Double-J Ranch. Nick's father.
Jordan, Darcy	Nick's Mother. Darcy Reeds married to Ben Jordan. Deceased.
Jordan, Nicholas	Aka, Nick. Friend and class mate of Jill Thomas.

-K-

Kast, Gill	Cadet Pilot of Apache Patrol Six, Class 1 Patrol Fighter.
Kiese, Prince	Warlord Prince of Knobaal.
Kiile	A Marine Squad Leader in the

services of the GPF. (Pronounced as Kī īle.) GPF Marine ID: USL15-EFM (Upper Squad Leader, Earth Force Marine)

Kooich, Hench; Major	A Shadow. Major in the GPF, commander of Q-KKLC14. GPF ID: RWKR17-SC.
Kooich, Leeana	Major Kooich's partner (wife). Lieutenant in the GPF, Nav-Com officer on Q-KKLC14. GPF ID: RWKR17-SC2.
Korveel, Director	Trader's Union Merchandise Director, under Senior Chairman Sorgat.
Kraast, Director	Trader's Union Intelligence Director, under Senior Chairman Sorgat.

-L-

Lima, Wally	State assigned Deputy to Riggin. Assigned to Riggin after Sheriff Black and his six deputies disappear. 26 yrs of age.
Lupis, Dan; Deputy	Special State Deputy assigned to Riggin under Wally Lima. Wife Mandy. Daughter Blaire (age 7).

-M-

Malone, Coleen	Married to Tom Reese (1), and to Brendan Cassel (2). GPF Planet-side ID: IAL01-SS. Registered Moira Geaardt.
Malone, Greg	Great Nephew to Gary Woods. Son of Coleen Reese (Malone). Stran Geaardt's registered birth name. Born March 17, same year as Shara Smallwood. GPF Terran ID: IAL02-SS
Malone, Shara (Shar)	Greg Malone's wife. Maiden name:

	Shara Smallwood. GPF Planet-side ID: IAL02 SS2.
Marks, Ted; Deputy	pecial Stat Deputy assigned to Riggin under Wally Lima.
Mary	Owner of Mary's Flower Boutique.
Matti	House girl at the Smallwood-Hawkins ranch.
McIntire, Doug	Significant friend of Rosalee (Rose) Mitchell's. (IAL38-SS)
Mitchell, Rosalee (Rose)	Friend of Shara Smallwood and Jill Thomas. Doug McIntire's significant friend. (IAL37-SS)
Moss, Wilm; Cadet	Cadet Pilot of Apache Patrol Four, Class 1 Patrol Fighter.

-P-

Parks, Chief	Police Chief in Hawthorne

-Q-

Q-STSX1	Colonel Stran Geaardt & Nav-Com Lieutenant Casi Geaardt. Campaign Commander for Trader's Union Offensive; Terran and non-terran forces.
Q-KKLC14	Major Hench Kooich & Nav-Com Lieutenant Leeana Kooich. Campaign Commander's lieutenant and Wing Commander under Colonel Geaardt.
Q-KVWC33	Major Daaws Miiles & Nav-Com Lieutenant Meecia Miiles
Q-LTVC21	Major Neel Glean & Lieutenant Debira Glean
Q-MKCC5	Major Aiilx Romaan & Lieutenant Colbee Donnr

Q-TTYF8	Major Mooren & Nav-Com, Lieutenant Franni Kaal
Q-LLRT12	Major Deni Bradg & Nav-Com Lieutenant Mri Bradg
Q-KCMM9	Major Pti Fila & Nav-Com Lieutenant Lori Tam
Q-JCCV4	Major Ronl Bids and Nav-Com Lieutenant Emly Bids. Joined Apache Squadron after supporting the attack of 4 January and getting repairs done at Obscure.
Q-QRTT7	Major Amel Clef and Nav-Com Lieutenant Pela Clef. Apache Squadron B-Group Wing Leaders.

-R-

Ranch Hands	At the Smallwood Ranch: Jimmy, Tom (Tommy), Billy and Dusty.
Reeds	Terran family name of the controlling Family in southern Riggs Valley.
Reeds, Bernice; Judge	Great Aunt of Shara Smallwood. Head operative in the Family affiliation with the Traders and Slavers. Riggs Valley Circuit Judge.
Reeds, Thad & Betti	A stranded couple that Wally helped on his way through Grants on his way back to Riggin (Dec 20). Son Sam, age thirteen, and daughter Glory, age nine.
Reese, Coleen	Married to Tom Reese (1), mother of Hew and (by an Affair) of Greg Malone. Maiden name: Coleen Malone.
Reese, Tom	Husband of Coleen (Malone). Distant relation of Gary Woods. GPF Planet-

	side ID: IAL01-SS2.
Riviera, Ensign	QuickSilver Tracnav Surveillance Specialist.
Russell, Chief	Chief of Police in Clay.
-S-	
Shara Malone	See Malone, Shara
Smallwood, Shara (Shar)	Unplanned daughter of Henry and Clea (Hawkins) Smallwood. Youngest of three. 28 yrs old. Born June 20 (solstice), same year as Greg Malone.
Smallwood, Henry	Full blooded Apache, American Indian. Married Clea Hawkins, father of Shara Smallwood.
STSX	Q-STSX1 is a late generation, Shadow Class Corvette, nicknamed as a type as Q-Ships, operated under the command of Stran Geaardt. The latest in the long evolution of the GPF's Shadow ships. The name is synonymous with the ship's central computer system ID.
-T-	
Thomas, Jack	Married Amy Woods, daughter of Gary Woods. Father of Jill. Financial Officer at the Woods Lumber Mill. (Father of Greg Malone by pre-marital affair with Coleen Reese.)
Thomas, Jill	Daughter of Jack Thomas and Amy Thomas (Woods). Six years younger than Shara Smallwood and Greg Malone.
Tigs, Ani; Cadet	Cadet Pilot of Apache Patrol Three, Class 2 Patrol Fighter.
Tina	Pert, brunette waitress at Hap's Place.

Townsley, Thomas, Colonel   Watch Commander, space station S.S. QuickSilver.

-W-

Wardly, Anne, Lt.   Staff Assistant and Aide to Admiral Baker, space station S.S. QuickSilver.

Woods, Harry   Son of Horace Woods. Longtime head of the Woods Lumber and Mill (Retired). Father of Gary, James and Brian.

Woods, Gary   Son of Harry Woods. Father of Bill Woods.

Woods, James   Son of Harry Woods. Father of Amy Woods.

Woods, Brian   Son of Harry Woods. Unmarried. Current head of the Woods Lumber and Mill.

Woods, Bill   Son of Gary Woods; no siblings. Father of Jim Woods, Lieutenant (USAF).

Woods, Jim, Lt.   Son of Bill Woods; no siblings. Married to Shelly Davis, father of Carrie Anne Woods.

Woods, Amy   Daughter of James Woods. Married to Jack Thomas, mother of Jill Thomas.

Places and Things:

-A-

Angrilat   A Principal commercial complex in the Kyddellan System

Antheria   Major Commercial Planet in the Tunst System. Known as a Heavy World with a gravity index of 2.02

	times Galactic Standard.
Aridont	City on Listera, cite of water rioting.

-B-

Baile	Planetary system of the planet Rygon.
Betolle	Planet in the Daneets System. Home planet of Lieutenant Franni Kaal and her hometown of Casimir.
Brekshiir	A wrist mounted laser weapon, consisting of one or multiple optics and fired by a unique sequence of mental commands. Specifically designed for the GPF Shadows.
	Brekshiir 170 Single Optic wrist Unit, 50 pulses with a range of 300 yds in air.
	Brekshiir 490 Wrist Clusters is the most common in the GPF, consisting of 4 laser units, 50 pulses each with a range of 300 yds in air. Individually fired or in combination.
	Brekshiir 710 Wrist Clusters, upgrade of the 490. 70 pulses with a range of 300 yds in air.
Brigstoan, Patrol Cruiser	GPF Patrol Cruiser designed for interception and boarding of suspect transports. Operated with a standard pilot crew, fifty aerial marines, a separate pilot crew and a Medical staff.

-C-

C.Date	A date referenced to the galactic calendar. A galactic year is comprised of one thousand galactic turns.

	Example: C.3482.329 is the 329th day of the galactic year 3284. It is also the 310th day of the current story year, November 6th.
Caldite Throwing Dart	A coveted and highly guarded GPF tool, used to inject a sedative or toxin upon impact.
Casimir	City on the planet Betolle, home town of Franni Kaal.
Cellystoan	Planetary system in which the Warlord Prince's home planet, Knobaal, orbits.
Centipar	One hundredth of a par. Similar to a terran minute.
Clay	Town in central Riggs Valley, 93 highway miles south of Riggin.
Corsecain	Planet in the Gashii system. Prominent for numerous bloody battles in the Moulit Wars.

-D-

Dangcee	Mining colony on the fourth planet of the Greel system.
Double J Ranch	A 43,138 Acre (67.4 sq. miles) horse ranch owned by Nick's father, Bob Jordan, situated between the North Butte and Riggin.

-G-

Galactic Peace Force	Galactic policing organization headquartered in the Gridelin Rings.
Galactic year	Equivalent to 1000 terran days, or 2.7397 standard terran years. See C.Date.
Grants	Town at the south end of Riggs Valley, 186 highway miles south of Riggin.

Greel System — Planetary system in which the Pico Mining Company has established numerous mining colonies.

Greymn — Major Industrial complex on Omerai Two, renowned for its weapons manufacture. Model 40 is hand weapon most widely used by the Trader's Guild.

Greymn Model 40: 40 destructive pulses with a range of 400 yds in air.

-H-

Hawthorne — Town in central Riggs Valley, 128 highway miles south of Riggin.

-I-

IFF — Identification, Friend or Foe. An identification system to determine if an entity, craft or forces are friendly, and to determine their bearing and range from the interrogator. The system is capable of transmitting a hail to another system on command.

-K-

Kaaspr — The standard issue brand of hand laser weapon for the Galactic Peace Force. Model 106 is the current standard laser hand weapon used in the GPF. Replaced the previous standard, Model 88.

Kaaspr Model 106: 50 destructive pulses with a maximum range of 350 yds in air.

Knobaal — Home planet and seat of the Royal Throne of the Warlord Prince Kiese. Located in the Cellystoan planetary system.

Kyddel	System in which Angrilat's home planet resides.
-L-	
Lazy D Ranch	Martin Davis' 15,455 acre ranch (24.15 sq miles).
-M-	
Millipar	One one-thousandth of a par. Similar to in concept but equivalent to 3.456 terran seconds.
-O-	
Omerai Two	Industrialized planet in the Kyddel system, noted for its arms manufacturing.
-P-	
Par	A fundamental galactic unit of time. Twenty-five pars in a Galactic Standard Turn (Day). Similar to a terran hour.
-Q-	
QuickSilver	Planet Earth's multinational, manned orbital space station. (S.S. QuickSilver.)
Q-Ships	Nickname for the Galactic Peace Force's two man Recondite Corvettes. Specifically used by Shadows in their various roles of information gathering, defense and protection.
-R-	
Riggin	A small college town in the northern point of Riggs Valley, western United States, planet Earth.
Rockin' H Ranch	A 1,263,950 Acre (1975 sq. mile) horse and cattle ranch belonging to Paul Hawkins and Nancy Hawkins

| | (deceased), situated NW of Riggin. |
| Rygon | Home planet of the very old Geaardt family name, located in the Baile System. |

-S-

| Shadow | Undercover agent of the Galactic Peace Force with specialized training and abilities in clandestine operations and information collecting, generally thought to be able to hide in plain sight. |
| Smallwood-Hawkins Ranch | Horse ranch belonging to Shara Malone (Smallwood). 209,275 Acres (approx. 327 sq. miles) split off of Paul Hawkins' larger ranch to its north. Situated West of Riggin. |

Books by Aidan Red

Paladin Shadow Series
Terran Assignment Triptych
Book 1: Things are not as they seem.
Book 2: When luck is not enough.
Book 3: Fate has a different idea.
Terran Recruits Triptych
Book 4: In the wake of chaos.
Book 5: Terran Talents join forces.
Book 6: New rules of engagement.
Operation Retribution Triptych
Book 7: The training phase.
Book 8: Taking the fight off-world.
Book 9: Luring the Prince into the open.
Garda Nua Triptych
Book 10: The proliferation of Talent.
Book 11: When a planet is stolen.
Book 12: Right does not ask permission.
Assignment: Casha-Six
Book 13: No Warning
Book 14: The Best Laid Plans
Book 14: A Change of Heart

Eight's Warning
Book 1: The Past Hunts.
Book 2: The Past Attacks.
Book 3: The Price of Escape.

More Books by Aidan Red

Keeper and His Tiger

Book 1: An Unexpected Complication.
Book 2: Deadly Undercurrents.
Book 3: The Trap.

Fearin' the Banshee

About the Author

Aidan Red's passion for aviation and aircraft design, engineering, and a deep interest in space and space travel go back many years. An avid reader from an early age, Aidan, with great trepidation, ventured into the world of writing during college. With real world experience in business aviation, Aidan's creative side led him to create an alternate world where the beautiful Riggs Valley was born and Shara's life became chronicled in his epic science fiction series, Paladin Shadows.

Paladin Shadows consists of the five triptychs (three-part works), *Terran Assignment, Terran Recruits, Operation Retribution, Garda Nua* and *Assignment: Casha-Six.* In between the Paladin triptychs, Aidan has penned two, three book series, *Keeper and his Tiger,* and *West's Ghost Ranch* and a novel, *Fearin' the Banshee.*

Unpublished books in his various series are scheduled for release on a regular basis in the coming months.

Visit *www.RedsInkandQuill.com* or *www.AidanRedBooks. com* for more information on Aidan Red's books and where to purchase them.

www.ingramcontent.com/pod-product-compliance
Lightning Source LLC
Chambersburg PA
CBHW070822180626
46818CB00001B/361